FOR THE PROTECTION OF A WOMAN

www.mascotbooks.com

For the Protection of a Woman

For more information, please contact:
Mascot Books, an imprint of Amplify Publishing Group
620 Herndon Parkway, Suite 320
Herndon, VA 20170
info@mascotbooks.com

Library of Congress Control Number: 2022912864

CPSIA Code: PRV0822A

ISBN-13: 978-1-63755-523-1

Printed in the United States

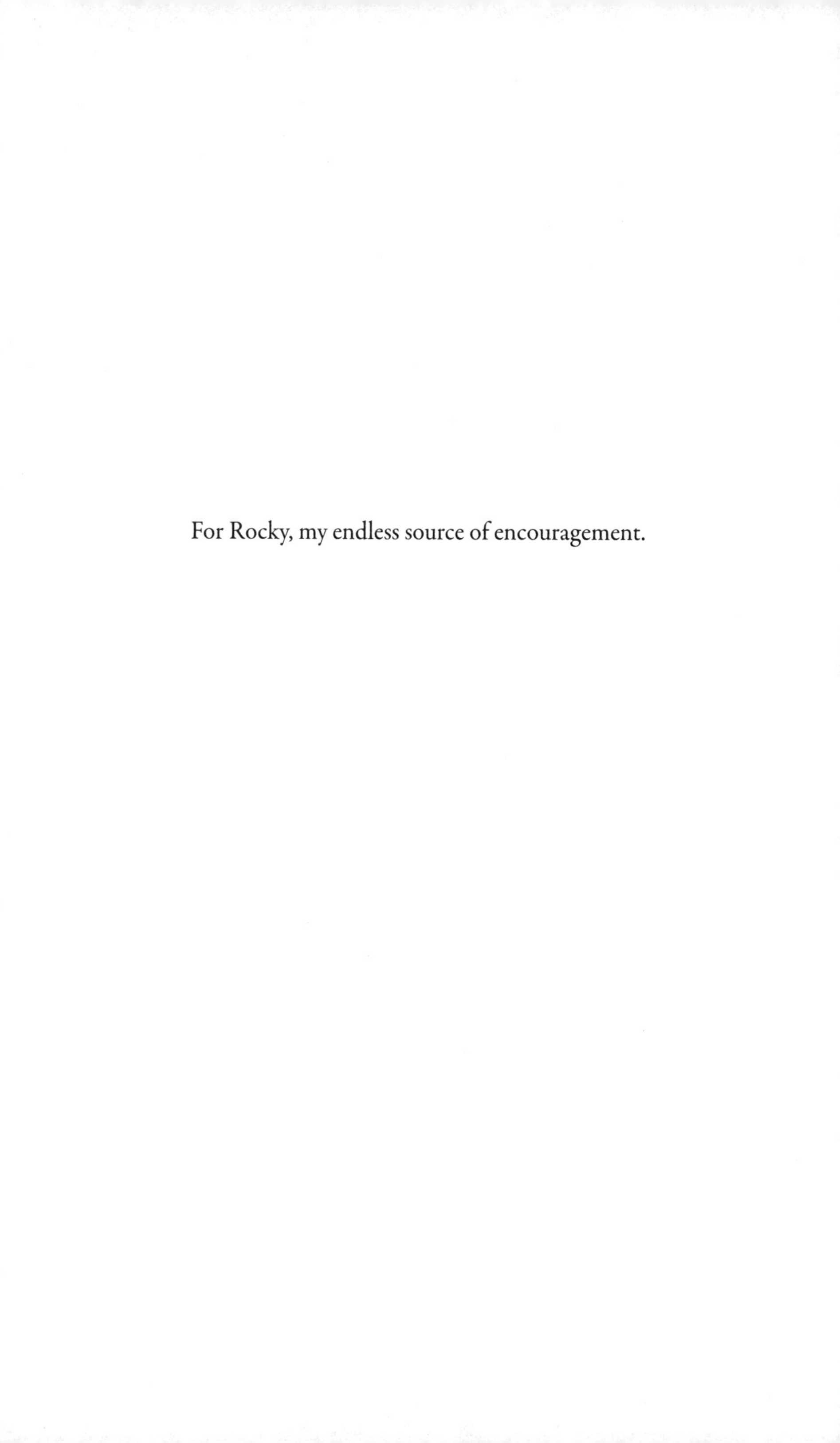

For Rocky, my endless source of encouragement.

FOR THE PROTECTION OF A WOMAN

KAT TAPPAN

CHAPTER ONE

FLEE TO THE COUNTRY

SARA HEARD A LOUD NOISE outside the front door. She removed her headphones and listened again. She heard someone trying to turn the doorknob. Sara remembered the safety rules her father had discussed and given to her to follow.

When someone is at the door trying to open it, first, do not open the door and do not ask who it is. Quietly proceed to the bathroom and hide in the large laundry hamper. Second, calling the police was not an option. Sara headed for the bathroom; it was down the hall from the living room, where she was listening to music. She shut the door and climbed into the large hamper and placed the clothes that were inside on top of her to hide herself. Third, quickly text Dad the situation at home. Sara always had her cell phone on her. She texted her dad that someone was trying to open the front door.

Sara was trying not to shake, but she was so scared; she was alone in the house. It was just her and her dad now; her mother had died from the Double X virus a few months ago. Her father went out this morning to try to get some food, which was harder and harder to come by. She remembered to turn down the ringer on her cell phone. Her dad returned the message. "On my way home, hide in the hamper." Sara heard a loud crash; someone had busted down the front door. She could hear things being tossed and thrown about the house.

She heard a man say, "See if there is any food in the kitchen, and I will search the rest of the house."

She could hear doors opening, glass breaking, and items hitting the floor. She heard a different man's voice saying, "There is some canned food, and I found some batteries. I will put them in the backpack."

She could hear someone ransacking each bedroom, then footsteps coming down the hall toward the bathroom. The door swung open, and someone entered. She put her hands over her mouth in an attempt to be very quiet and still. She could tell he was going through the medicine cabinet, as she could hear pill bottles rattling. She couldn't see the man, but she could smell him, and he did not smell good.

"I found some medications and some aspirin!" the man yelled.

She could then hear him talking quietly to himself. "Toothpaste, bandages, peroxide—these will be useful." Then she heard the sound of the shower curtain being pushed open and shampoo bottles hitting the bottom of the tub.

"Someone is here! We better get the hell out of here!" the man from the kitchen yelled.

She heard the men run out the back door into the backyard. She heard the garage door to the house open, and someone came inside.

"Hello? Anybody here? I'm armed."

Sara's father, Will, stood beside the garage door with a large knife. He walked to the kitchen, the living room, and down the hall while holding the knife out in front of him. He noticed that the house had been rummaged through. He saw and heard no one. He entered the bathroom and lifted the lid of the laundry hamper. He pulled the clothes off Sara's head and looked down at her; she had tears in her eyes. Will reached down and grabbed her hand and helped her out. Sara began to cry uncontrollably.

"Don't ever leave me home alone again! I hate you for leaving me!"

Will grabbed Sara and hugged her. She began to hit him with her fists in the chest. He grabbed her little hands.

"Sara, it's OK. You're safe now. I'm not going to leave you."

Sara laid her head on his chest. "I'm sorry, Daddy."

Will knew at that moment they could not remain in the city; it was just getting too dangerous to remain. The city had become an unsafe place for a ten-year-old girl.

Sara was born in Des Moines and had never lived anywhere but the city. Will grew up on a farm near the town of Jefferson, which was a couple of hours' drive outside Des Moines. He had moved to the city to attend college, and that was where he met and married Sara's mother. But now Will and Sara were alone since her mother passed of the virus. As the population of females in the city started to get ill, people started to panic. The government started to restrict women's movement to try to contain the virus. Soon the city government restricted the female population to remain in the city, in an attempt to keep the virus out of the rural areas. There were law enforcement patrols in the streets to keep the women confined to their homes, and the CDC started a mask mandate for females. Schools closed, businesses started to shut down, Will's place of employment laid everyone off until further notice. Grocery stores were running out of supplies. Everyone was panic buying everything till the shelves were empty.

After Will had gotten Sara settled down, he sat her at the kitchen table. He proceeded to put the front door back up. He boarded it up with some two-by-fours he had in the garage.

"Dad, I am hungry." Sara rubbed her stomach.

"I know, honey. I wasn't able to get anything today. Stores are just empty, and the people that broke in today took everything we had."

Will knew what he had to do; he had no other choice but to try to contact his brother, Rick.

Will's elder brother, Rick, resided at the family farm. Rick and his wife, Kate, had moved back to the farm a couple of years ago when he retired from the military. Their elderly parents were getting to the point they needed help to run the farm. Kate was a registered nurse and worked part time at the small hospital in the nearby town of Jefferson. Will had not spoken to Rick since he had moved back to the farm. They did not get along, even as children. Rick always said they stopped speaking to each other over a misunderstanding regarding their parents and the farm. Will knew it was because Rick blamed him for the accidental drowning of their sister, Amy, many years ago when they were children. Will didn't have Rick's current cell phone number, so he would try his parents' landline.

After Sara was off to bed, Will tried his parents' phone. Cell service was spotty these days. "This number is currently unavailable," the message stated. He tried the number again, same message. Will went into the living room and sat down, his elbows on his knees and his head in his hands. He needed to decide. Should he continue to try to call his brother or just pack up and take the chance and go straight to the farmhouse? He looked over at the boarded-up front door. He needed to get Sara out of the city; it just was not safe, and there were no more food resources.

Will had heard that to leave the city, they needed to pass through a law enforcement checkpoint. Females in the city were advised to stay indoors and to register with the city. Women were told to stay within the city limits for their protection by city officials. Will assumed the checkpoints were to look for females trying to leave the city. Will quietly packed a bag for him and Sara—clothes, hygiene products, and bottles of water. He stood in the living room with his hands on his hips and looked around his home, now in shambles. He had worked so hard to own his own home. Now he had to leave it. This had been the only home that Sara had ever known, and he was going to ask her to leave it too.

He walked into her room and gently shook her shoulder. "Sara, wake up."

Sara woke, rubbed her eyes, and said, "What's the matter, Dad?"

Will looked at her and explained that they needed to leave their home and go to the family farm. Sara had only been to the farm when she was a baby, so she had no memory of ever being there or any memory of her grandparents.

"Farm?" Sara looked puzzled.

"Yes, I told you about Grandma and Grandpa Campbell's farm, the one I grew up on."

She nodded. "Yes, I remember now. Can't we stay here? I don't want to go."

"It is not safe here anymore, Sara. We must go. Now get dressed."

Sara frowned and stomped her feet as she got dressed in the clothes Will had left out for her.

"What about my stuff, Dad? What can I bring?" she yelled down the hall.

"We will just bring what we need. We will leave everything else for now. I have already packed your bag."

"Can I bring my tablet with my music?" He nodded yes.

Will helped Sara put on her jacket. He knew leaving at night might be a better plan. Less people around, less cars on the road. He would tell the officers at the checkpoint that he was on his way to his parents' house out near Jefferson. They both walked out to the garage, where the car was parked. Will stopped. How was he going to hide Sara? What if they searched the car? He opened the trunk and looked inside; there were jumper cables, a flashlight, an umbrella, and a blanket.

"Sara, you're going to need to hide in the trunk. I will have you get toward the back, and then I will put all these things in front of you to hide you from view."

She looked at her father and then at the trunk and then back at him.

"I don't want to ride in the trunk, Dad. You are scaring me!"

Will pulled the items out of the trunk.

"Sara, this is for your protection. We need to pass through a checkpoint. I do not want the officers to find you. I feel that this is the safest way to go. Besides, you do not have a choice."

Will pointed at the trunk and nodded at Sara. She reluctantly climbed inside the trunk. Will placed all the items around Sara, including the bags that he had packed. He closed the trunk and looked toward the sky, praying that they would not ask to look inside the trunk and, if they did, they would not discover Sara.

Will climbed into the car, took a deep breath, and started the engine. As he pulled out of the garage and out into the driveway, he could see a figure move in the shadows and then run up to the car. "Do you have any food? Hey, any food?" The man pounded on the window. Will shook his head as he pulled out of the driveway and onto the street with the man yelling and screaming at him as he drove away. Sara was crying in the trunk; she was trying to be as quiet as she could. Her heart was pounding and her hands shaking. She wished it could all be over.

Will continued driving, trying to use the quickest route to get out of town and onto the highway. The streetlights flickered off and on. He could see that the east side of town was black and that the power was out. Garbage blew in the wind along the streets. He could see a couple of cars off in the distance that were on fire. He looked at his gas gauge, and he was estimating that he should just have enough gas to get to the farm, at least he was hoping. He continued to drive. As he rolled down his window, he could hear gunfire. His eyes darted back and forth, looking for any signs of danger.

Sara also was listening; she was trying to be brave. Her stomach was turning with nausea, riding in the trunk was making her carsick. She hated not being able to see what was going on, but she did feel safer hiding in the trunk. Sara's life had changed so much in the last couple of months. Some of her friends got sick, and some had died. Her own mother was now gone. First, school was shut down, then no playing outside, then it was harder to text her friends. She began to feel isolated.

She could feel the car slowing down and could hear people talking in the distance. The voices got louder, then the car stopped. She tried to hear what the voices were saying. She felt the car move forward and then stop again.

"Sara," her father said softly, "I need you to be very quiet and try not to move."

He did not want her to be found. He drove up to the checkpoint, his heart racing. Will stopped as the officer approached the driver of the vehicle in line in front of him. He couldn't hear what they were saying, but he could see the driver shaking his head, then the guards motioned for the driver to step out of his vehicle. One officer frisked the driver while the other inspected the vehicle. The second officer stepped back from the vehicle, pulled his weapon, and commanded, "Get out of the vehicle!"

A woman climbed out of the car.

"Lie down on the ground," he added.

A third officer approached Will.

"Where are you traveling to, sir?" Will looked up at the officer.

"Heading for my dad's place out in Gentry Valley. He is old and needs my help."

The officer was paying more attention to the activity with the driver in front of them.

"OK." He motioned him to drive around. "Be on your way."

Will put the car in drive and carefully drove around and accelerated, watching in the rearview mirror as the checkpoint got smaller and smaller until finally, he relaxed and took a big breath. He continued several miles just to be sure, then, when he felt it was safe, pulled over. He got out and opened the trunk.

"Sara, are you all right?" he asked.

"I don't feel well at all, Dad," she said shakily.

"We made it through the checkpoint. We'll be at Uncle Rick's soon."

He helped Sara out of the trunk and around to the back seat, where he had her lie down out of view. The sun was just starting to rise. Sara lay quietly, looking up at the top of the car, as they traveled. She wondered what Uncle Rick and Aunt Kate were like. She had never met them, and her father rarely ever spoke about them. Were they going to be glad to meet her? Were they nice? Mean? As thoughts danced in her head, she finally fell asleep.

*****

Will had been driving about an hour. He had seen no one else on the road. He turned on the car radio and tuned it to the only station he found that was giving a signal. "The death toll of the Double X pandemic stands at 96 percent of the world's female population. Cell service remains limited, and local hospitals remain closed. Rioters continue to take to the streets daily. Women and girls are strongly advised to seek safety." He turned the radio off; things were getting continually worse. He was hoping that his family was still alive. Were his mother and sister-in-law alive?

Will started to worry about his gas tank; the needle was on empty. He was keeping his fingers crossed they would at least get close enough to walk the rest of the way.

"We're almost there," he said to Sara, who replied only with a moan.

It had been years since Will had been to the farm. He recalled memories of growing up there, some good, some bad. The sun had finally risen as they reached the gravel road leading down to the farmhouse. A couple of miles down the road, they reached a locked gate. Will stopped and got out of the car. Sara sat up in the back seat. A big metal gate was shut and locked with a large padlock. Will came up and opened the back door of the car.

"Well, Sara, it looks like we are walking the rest of the way. We were about to run out of gas anyway."

She got out of the car, and Will opened the trunk and grabbed their bags.

"Is it far, Dad?" Sara asked as Will tossed the bags over the gate.

"Oh, about a half mile or so," he answered as he helped her climb over the gate.

Will and Sara arrived at the front porch of the farmhouse. It was a two-story house painted white, and it had a white picket fence surrounding the yard and the house. The front porch reached the entire length of the front of the house. On the porch were a couple of chairs and a wooden bench. It was an old house but had many upgrades. Solar panels that Rick had added since the power would go out often in storms could be seen. Down from the house toward the pasture was a large barn, a corral, some fruit trees, and a large space for a garden. The house was on twenty acres and had been in the family for a long time. Their family had grown hay and corn there for many years. Will knocked and tried the doorknob, which was locked.

"Rick! Are you there? This is Will."

When Rick heard the knock on the door, he immediately turned to Kate.

She was already descending the stairs to the basement. She turned the lights off when she reached the bottom of the stairs and settled herself in the darkness of the basement. This had become an automatic reaction for Kate anytime someone came to the door or was seen on the property. Rick did not want anyone to know she was still alive. It was a large basement set up in different sections, one with a cot, a chair, a table, and several cabinets with various medical supplies. Across the room was a desk, a bookcase with books, and a root cellar in the other corner. They had heard rumors that females were being asked to register with the county because of the Double X virus taking the life of so many of the population, in this case those with two X chromosomes, females. Coughing, sneezing, or simply touching a contaminated surface spread the virus, and it spread throughout the country and eventually the world. As it did, fear set in—of there being no more females to continue the human race. They never had time to complete a vaccine.

For reasons that were not clear, there were some women whose DNA afforded them a natural immunity to the virus. Kate was one of those women. While working at the hospital, unlike her female coworkers, she never became ill. Her male coworkers started eyeing her suspiciously and talking behind her back. One day she overheard one of the doctors stating they needed to get a sample of her blood and DNA. She called Rick, who instructed her to leave immediately. She went to the supply room, grabbing as many medical supplies as she could—bandages, gauze, saline—whatever she could stash in her bag, then to the medication cabinet before scurrying out to her car. She cried the entire way home, not out of sadness but out of fear and anxiety. Now she no longer went to work, and Rick had told them that she had caught the virus and passed away. Kate mainly stayed out of sight or dressed herself as a man to not be discovered.

Rick peeked through the foyer window and saw Will standing there with a child.

"Will, what the hell are you doing here?" Rick yelled through the window.

Will tried the door again. "Rick, unlock the door. It is not safe for Sara in the city anymore. I need your help!"

"Does she have the virus?" Rick replied, concerned for Kate.

"No! Please help us," Will pleaded.

Kate had heard the conversation and came back up from the basement.

"Let them in, Rick, for God's sake!" Kate demanded.

She pushed by Rick and opened the door.

"Come in." Kate brought the two in. "Please sit down." Kate led them into the living room.

"Where is Mom and Dad?" Will asked, looking around the room. Will repeated himself, "Where is Mom and Dad?"

Will ran to the kitchen and then upstairs, looking everywhere for his parents. He then went down to the basement. Kate followed him down.

Rick and Sara stood there looking at each other. Sara took a seat on the couch.

"Are you my uncle Rick?" Rick just glared and said nothing.

"Will!" yelled Kate. He stopped and turned and looked at Kate. He had tears in his eyes. He already knew the answer to his question.

"When did they pass?" he asked.

Kate let him know that his mother acquired the virus. She tried everything but could not save her, and she passed away about a month ago. His father followed soon after. She felt he died of a broken heart. He could not bear to live without his "sweet Maggie," as he called her. Both his parents were buried out near the flower garden that his mother loved so dearly.

"I'm so sorry, Will. I loved your parents very much. They were always so kind to me."

She reached out to hug him, and he pulled away.

"They were good people," he said as he returned upstairs to the living room, where Rick stood with his face red and his fists clenched.

"You've got a lot of nerve coming here! You have not spoken to me or our parents in two years!"

Sara sat there with her eyes filled with fear. Kate came over to her and sat down next to her on the couch. She looked into Sara's eyes, seeing she was scared. She brushed the hair from Sara's face. Rick gave her a disapproving look, to which Kate replied by angrily gesturing him away until he had retreated out the front door.

"Sorry you had to leave your home, but you are welcome here. This is your family's home. I am your aunt Kate. It is nice to meet you."

Kate reached out her hand to Sara.

"I'm Sara," she replied as she shook Kate's hand.

"I bet you're hungry. I have some apples in the kitchen."

Kate took Sara and Will into the kitchen. She gestured for Sara to sit down at the kitchen table, which was the center point of the room. The kitchen in the old farmhouse was large. It had both an old stove that burned wood and a newer electric stove. There were many cabinets and cupboards and a large kitchen sink. There were windows facing the backyard and a door that led to the large back porch. It had wallpaper of tiny yellow flowers on the walls. A bowl of apples was in the center of the table. Sara grabbed one and began to eat. Will took the opportunity to talk with Kate.

"It is nice to see you, Kate. It has been a long time." Kate motioned Will over to the corner of the kitchen so Sara would not hear their conversation.

"Will, tell me what is going on in the city. We are isolated out here in the country, and TV and radio are almost nonexistent."

At that point Rick had returned and heard Kate's question to Will.

"Yes, we would be interested in knowing what is going on," Rick interjected.

Will told them how the virus had spread fast through the city and that his wife had also passed away. His employer had shut down, stores were pretty much empty, people had become desperate, and city officials had instructed all females to not leave the city.

"Will, I am sorry you lost your wife. Sara must be devastated." Kate reached out and touched Will's hand. Will looked down.

"Yes, Sara's life has been turned upside down."

For a ten-year-old girl, Sara had been very responsible, caring for her mother in her last days and quickly mastering all the "safety rules" Will had set up to protect her from the outside world, including keeping quiet, closing the curtains, and staying indoors. He thought of her thin build, dark hair, and brown eyes—just like her mother's—and her smart, sweet, and sometimes smart-ass personality. He loved her silly sense of humor, how she would read every book twice, and the way she would immerse herself in her music on her iPod. He felt relieved they had made it to the old farmhouse.

Rick paced back and forth in the kitchen. "What about the federal government? Who is running the country?"

"It pretty much has become martial law in the city. There are disruptions in power and cell phone service. Many are trying to leave the city. They have set up checkpoints on each road leading out of the city. I had to hide Sara in the trunk of my car. We were so lucky to make it through. We had nowhere to go but here. I need a safe place for Sara."

Will looked over at Sara eating another apple. The farm could offer her a roof over her head and food for her stomach. They had the capability to grow their own fruits and vegetables, a couple of steer to eat, and fresh water from the well. More protection with more people to keep an eye on her. He knew he was the last person his brother wanted to see, but this was about protecting Sara, not about him.

"Rick, I know we have never seen eye to eye, but this is about my daughter, your niece. She needs a safe place to stay, please!" Rick again began to pace back and forth.

Kate stopped him in his tracks. "Rick, they are family. This is their home too. I would really like for Sara to stay. She would be safe here."

"I could never leave her here without me, but I want to do what is right for her," Will explained.

"This is not his home anymore, but our parents would not want me to turn away their grandchild." Rick looked over at Sara staring at him.

Kate put her hand on Will's shoulder and waited until his gaze met hers.

"We would never ask you to leave behind your daughter, would we, Rick?" Kate looked at Rick.

"That is another mouth to feed!" he said sternly.

"That is true, but we would have more help to plant and work the farm," Kate returned, having anticipated his reply. "And you could use Will's help in the fields. Sara can help in the garden. You have always told me Will is a good mechanic. Maybe he can get the tractor running?" She looked lovingly into Rick's eyes. "Please, Rick."

Rick could not resist that look. He wanted her to be happy, but he also wanted her to be safe. Having more people around to make mistakes could jeopardize her safety.

"We'll give it *one* month," he said unwillingly. "There will be extra chores to do, and everyone will have to work hard or be asked to leave." They all agreed.

CHAPTER TWO

SETTLING IN

KATE TOOK SARA TO ONE of the bedrooms upstairs. It had two big windows that looked down to the small orchard of apple and peach trees. The curtains were blue.

"Sara, I am going to ask you to please leave the curtains closed."

Sara interrupted, "I know, so no one will see me." Kate looked over at Sara, who had her arms crossed over her body.

"It seems you had a few rules at your house in the city. What other rules did your dad have for you to follow?"

Will had told Sara not to open the door if someone knocked or ask who it was but to hide and wait. She had to remain in the house and could not go outside. She could listen to music but only if it was with her headphones. She was to remain quiet.

"Those sound like good rules. We have a few rules around here, but we like to call them safety precautions. But we will go over those here a little later."

Kate proceeded to show Sara around her room. There was a double bed with a comforter with big blue flowers spread across it. There were a dresser, a lamp beside the bed, and a little desk in the corner. The walls were painted white with paintings of horses hung on them.

"Your grandmother loved horses," Kate explained.

"I love them too!" Sara said with a moment of excitement.

"Good. Go ahead and get settled in. You could put your clothes in the dresser. When you're done, come get me. I will be in my room just down the hall."

Kate left Sara in her room and went into her and Rick's room down the hall. Their room was painted a light blue. Kate had hung pictures of family on one of the walls, and there was a clock on the opposite wall. She had various knickknacks on her dresser. She flopped herself down on the bed. She put her hands to her head and sighed a big sigh. Kate had a million thoughts whirling around her mind. There was so much she needed to do now that there were two more people in the home, especially with one being a child. She knew the first thing she had to do was to teach Sara the safety precautions that she and Rick had established. She would start with a tour of the house and property, explaining the rules along the way. Kate thought there were many things Sara would need to learn; the world was changing, and Sara would need to learn some survival skills.

There was a woodstove in the old farmhouse she would need to learn to light and cook with and a well from which she would need to learn to draw water. She would need to learn how to manage when the power went out and they needed to rely on their limited solar power. Sara would also need to learn how to provide first aid and, as she got older, CPR, cleaning a wound, and suturing a laceration. *Let's not get ahead of myself,* Kate thought. At that point Sara came into Kate's room.

"I'm finished." Sara sat down beside Kate on the bed. "Aunt Kate, did you know my mom?"

"No, Sara, I did not. Your dad and uncle Rick haven't gotten along for a very long time, so we never came to visit. I would have liked to have gotten to know her. Maybe you can tell me about her if you like." Kate placed her hand on Sara's shoulder.

"Maybe someday." Sara looked up at Kate, smiling.

"Well, let's start with a tour of the farm. Let me see, you have jeans and a T-shirt on. That will work. Let's add a cap that we can put your hair under. We need to disguise ourselves as boys, for our safety."

Kate grabbed a cap from her closet and helped Sara put her long brown hair under the hat. Then Kate started the tour. First, she showed

Sara around the upstairs. There were four bedrooms and a bathroom. As they were going through the rooms, they found Will in one bedroom putting his things away. He had taken the big bedroom that had a balcony. It was his parents' bedroom when he was a child.

"Will, I am giving Sara a tour of the house and farm. Would you like to join us?"

Will pulled on a pair of cowboy boots. "I am going to go see Rick and get some things worked out, but please continue the tour." Will winked at Sara as he went down the stairs.

He headed down to the barn to see if Rick was there. The barn had wide doors and stalls for the animals and a hayloft at the top. Rick was inside, milking the cow. Will walked up beside him.

"First, let me say thank you for letting Sara and I stay," Will started, "and let me reassure you we will pull our own weight."

"I just don't want any of your bullshit," Rick retorted. "This is for a month trial, and I am sure you will most likely fuck it up." Rick stood up and stood toe to toe with Will.

Will poked Rick in the chest. "There you go, expecting the worst of me before we even get started."

"Well, you could start by seeing if you can repair the tractor," Rick offered.

"OK, I'll see what I can do," Will replied, heading for the tractor. "Do we have any gas?"

Rick showed him the gas cans. "This is all we have, so we don't want to waste it."

*****

Will got started on the tractor. After an hour of cussing and throwing tools, Will headed back to the house to get a glass of water. While in the kitchen, he heard laughing. It was coming from the basement. He paused at the top of the stairs to listen.

"So they could see your black bra through your white shirt?" Sara giggled.

"Yes, but I didn't notice until I went to the bathroom to check my hair, and then I saw it!" They both laughed. "So you see, Sara, we all get embarrassed sometimes. It's just part of life."

On that note Will came through the door. "Well, it seems you two are getting along."

"Yes, we are," Kate answered.

"Aunt Kate is cutting my hair. I said I would be embarrassed to have it too short," Sara explained, "so Aunt Kate was telling me about how it is to be really embarrassed."

With a raised voice, Will said, "Kate, why are you cutting her beautiful hair?"

Will grabbed Kate's hand that had the scissors. Kate stepped away from Sara and tried to free her hand from Will's grip; he let go. Kate put the scissors down.

"I'm so sorry, Will. I should have checked with you first. If Sara is going to go outside at all, she needs to look more like a boy than a girl. It was hard getting all her hair under the cap, so I asked if I could cut it," Kate explained.

"Dad, I said it was OK. Mom had short hair. I don't like it when you get mad and yell," Sara scolded. Will squatted down to face Sara.

"I'm sorry, sweetheart. I should not have yelled at Aunt Kate. How about you let me in on discussions? I'm your dad and would like to know what is going on." Will looked up at Kate, who nodded yes.

"OK, but no yelling. You didn't like it when Mom yelled at us," said Sara, pointing her finger at Will.

"OK, you got a deal." Will shook Sara's hand.

They heard the kitchen door slam. "Will, where the hell are you?" Rick shouted.

Will looked at Kate and rolled his eyes. "He is already yelling at me."

Will turned and returned upstairs. "Yes, Rick, what's up?"

"How come the tractor is not working?" he asked sharply.

"It all checks out, except for the fuel filter," Will explained. "I'll start with trying to clean it, but it may need to be replaced."

"What are you doing in the house?" Rick said loudly, on purpose, so Kate would hear him.

"Well, if you don't mind"—Will smirked—"I came in for a drink of water and to check on my child."

"OK, well, get back to work," Rick said as he headed out the door.

Kate came up behind Will. "Wow, he has it in for you, doesn't he?" Kate tried not to judge Will by his brother's rants. He obviously loved his child, and that was a plus in her book.

"It's been like that since we were kids," Will said, getting another drink of water. "I am done trying to appease him."

"Well, if you want to stick around, I suggest you appease him the best you can," Kate said, patting him on the shoulder.

"I'll try," Will said, rolling his eyes before heading back out to the tractor.

After cleaning the fuel filter, the tractor started right up.

"Hot damn!" Will shouted as he drove the tractor out of the barn.

"Holy hell, you did it!" Rick exclaimed, waving his hat at Will. "Now planting can get started."

As Will and Rick were celebrating, they did not notice two men walking up the driveway and heading for the front door of the house.

Sara and Kate were still down in the basement. Kate had just finished showing Sara where all the medical supplies were kept. She was now showing her the root cellar and how they used it to store some kinds of food.

"We keep a lot of fruits and vegetables in here. I have a box of apples upstairs I need to put in here. I will be right back. I am going to go get them."

Kate started up the basement stairs to the kitchen. As she reached for the box of apples, she heard a knock on the front door, then the sound of someone turning the doorknob.

"Hey, is anybody home?" the stranger called out as Kate quickly retreated to the basement stairs, closing the door behind her. "Anybody home?" the stranger repeated.

Kate snuck down the stairs as quietly as possible and into the basement.

"Sara, come with me," she whispered sharply as she grabbed Sara's hand. She opened the door of a large armoire up against the wall. "Get in," she instructed.

Sara climbed in, and Kate came in after and shut the armoire door. Kate then slid open a fake back door to the armoire and motioned for Sara to step into the small space barely big enough for them both. Kate closed the door as they heard footsteps on the stairs. At that moment they heard Rick say, "Can I help you? You know you are trespassing."

At the top of the stairs, Will stood next to Rick, who was holding his shotgun. The men turned around. They were well dressed and clean and had no weapons that they could see, which did not mean they were not carrying.

"Sorry, we were just here conducting a census. The governor is trying to get a handle on how many residents we have left in the county and what food resources there are," the men explained. "Also informing every one of the 8:00 p.m. curfew," the men added.

"What governor?" Rick asked.

"The acting governor, Paul Morrison," they answered.

"Self-appointed, you mean," Rick retorted. "Well, there is just the two of us here."

"Wait a moment." One of the men paused.

"Aren't you Rick Campbell, and don't you have a wife?"

"I did," Rick replied in his best effort to sound sullen. "But she passed several months ago from the virus. If you like," he continued, "I can show you her grave out back, for your census."

"No, that's not necessary," the men replied. "We'll just be on our way. Thank you for your cooperation." The two men passed by Rick and Will on the stairs and went out the front door.

Will and Rick watched as the two men walked back down the driveway. Will turned to go down to the basement, but Rick grabbed his arm.

"Wait," he said, still watching out the doorway as he held on to Will. "I want to make sure they are gone before we tell them it's OK to come out." Rick now stepped back and closed the door but kept looking around the curtains for any signs of movement.

"Do you really have a grave out back?" Will asked, befuddled.

"Of course," Rick replied. "You can't be too careful."

Down in the basement, Sara and Kate waited breathlessly in the back of the armoire. Finally, they heard someone coming down the stairs.

"Kate, it's OK to come out now," Rick said, sliding open the door to where she and Sara were hidden. Sara ran out straight to her father.

"I was so scared, Daddy," Sara said, bursting into tears.

"Don't worry, it's all right now," he said, comforting her. Will stepped closer to the armoire and looked inside. "So that is where you were hiding!" he said before turning to Rick in genuine admiration. "Great idea."

"So what happened up there?" Kate asked as she took a seat at the table. "Did you not see those men coming to the house?" Rick explained how Will got the tractor running, and they were distracted.

"By the time we saw the men," he concluded, "they were already at the porch."

"Good thing you had your plan in place," Will said.

"Though we may want to make some adjustments," Kate redirected. "If I hadn't happened to go upstairs right at that moment, we wouldn't have known the men were there until they were halfway down to the basement. They would have surely heard us, and we wouldn't have had any chance to make it to the armoire to hide."

"You're right," Rick agreed. "We need protocol for just this kind of situation. Things have changed now that we have a child here."

The four of them sat at the table and discussed different emergency situations and what was the best way to handle them. Strangers arriving on the property unannounced, intruder in the house or on the property, doors needing to be locked at all times, appropriate places for Sara to hide, the need for Sara to know how to ride a horse and even how to handle a gun. While the adults talked and planned, Sara sat there with wide eyes. Kate noticed her concern.

"Don't worry, Sara, I will go over all these situations with you so you will know exactly what to do. Just like your dad had rules at your other house, we will have them here also for your and our safety."

"I want to go home!" Sara shouted.

Will turned toward Sara, putting his forehead on hers, and softly said, "I know you're scared, sweetheart, and I understand. I am scared too. That is why we want you to learn all these things to help protect you. I know this is not your home, but it can be in time. Give it a chance."

Sara, through her tears, said, "OK." Kate came over and gave Sara a tissue so she could wipe her face.

"We can talk about this more later," Rick said before getting up from the table. "For now, I need to get back out to the barn." He gave Kate an irritated look as he went upstairs.

As Rick left, Will stayed to reassure Sara, and Kate went upstairs to her bedroom.

Shortly after Kate went to her room upstairs, Will came up and politely knocked.

"Kate, can I come in?"

"Sure, what can I help you with?" Kate replied.

"I just want to apologize for my behavior regarding cutting Sara's hair. I should have never grabbed you the way I did. I'm sorry." Will looked down at the floor.

Kate walked over to Will and placed her hand on his shoulder.

"Thank you, Will. I appreciate the apology. I know that things have been rough for you and Sara. I can't imagine what you have been through. Let's just start over. Hello, how are you? My name is Kate." She laughed.

"That sounds like a good plan, and I am doing better now." Will smiled at Kate, and she winked back at him. Will did not know Kate very well; it had been many years since he had even seen her. He did remember she was a kind, caring, and creative person, and she had a great smile. She had short reddish-brown hair and green eyes and stood on the short side.

Kate watched Will as he left the room and went downstairs. She thought about what a handsome man he was and how he and Rick looked alike but were so different. Will seemed to be a good father. Kate had no experience with children except at the hospital. She had no children of her own. She liked the idea of having Sara around but obviously had a lot to learn, and she now had a lot to teach.

CHAPTER THREE

TEACHING

A COUPLE OF WEEKS HAD gone by since Will and Sara had arrived at the farm. Kate had spent a lot of the last two weeks teaching and guiding Sara in the processes of the farm, but most importantly teaching what she needed to know about being safe. She was now well versed in all the places to hide on the property. Everyone now knew to whistle if strangers were noticed, which would signal Sara and Kate to hide. They had hung an old dinner bell down by the barn. Then if Sara and Kate were in the house, Will or Rick could ring the bell to warn of danger. Sara had learned to light a fire in the old woodstove and how to operate the well by hand. Kate had begun teaching her how to take care of the horses and was teaching her to ride. Sara loved the horse but still had an uneasy feeling around them.

"That will go away with time, and soon enough you will be a good rider," Kate reassured. "How about you try without me leading the horse? Just take her around the corral."

Kate let go of the reins and nodded at Sara. She started around the corral, walking at first, then trotting.

"Hey, look at me!" Sara shouted.

"Yes, you are getting the hang of it now!" Kate praised.

After a good ride around the corral, Kate and Sara brushed, fed, and watered the horses and returned to the farmhouse.

There was one more important lesson Sara needed to learn, and that was to handle a firearm. When Sara came back inside the house,

Will was sitting at the kitchen table with some bottles, a cloth, and a disassembled revolver.

"Why do you have a gun?" Sara asked curiously.

"I'm getting it ready to teach you how to handle it," Will answered, glancing up for a moment to look Sara in the eye. "There are evil people in the world, and you need to be prepared."

"You told me to never touch your gun, Dad," Sara said, taking a step back.

"Don't worry, I'm going to teach you everything you need to know about how to handle yourself."

"OK," Sara said.

"First," Will said, having reassembled the weapon, "when looking at or holding a gun, always consider it to be loaded. Next, keep your finger off the trigger until you're ready to shoot. Last, whenever you're holding a gun, make sure to point it in a safe direction, and when you aim, aim only at what you intend to shoot."

Will let those ideas sink in for a moment before continuing.

"This particular gun is a revolver." He continued, demonstrating as he spoke. "You see if it's loaded by releasing the cylinder and rotating it to the side. Here, I want you to try."

Sara took the gun into her hands and held it as he had instructed. Then she released the cylinder and rotated it to the side.

"Look," Will said as he showed her, "it's empty."

"When do I get to shoot it?" Sara inquired.

"We're heading outside for some target practice right now."

Sara followed Will outside and down to the barn. He had already set up a target in front of a couple of hay bales. He then instructed Sara on how to use the gun's sights to aim the gun at the target. Next, he gave her the gun and showed her how to stand. He instructed as he helped her raise the gun to eye level before letting go.

"Now take a deep breath, aim, and shoot."

Sara pulled the trigger. The sound of the gun cracked through the air as the bullet missed the target.

"I missed!" Sara said disappointedly.

"It will take some practice to get better. Let's try again," Will reassured her.

After some time practicing with the gun, Sara returned to the house, where Kate was cooking in the kitchen.

"So are you ready to help me with dinner?" she asked as Sara took off her jacket.

"What are you going to cook today?" she asked.

"We are preparing these carrots I got from our garden and a nice pot of beans." Kate put on an apron.

"Where is one for me?" Sara asked.

Kate reflected for a moment. "You know, we just might have to make you one. I am pretty sure there is an old sewing machine up in the attic. We can go up there later and look."

Will had returned to the fields. Rick was driving the tractor, and Will was starting to plant. Most of the fields were for hay and grain for the cattle and horses. The farm was about twenty acres, and the Gentry River bordered the back of the property. Their family had been selling hay and grain to cattle ranchers for many years. They had a large vegetable garden directly behind the house, along with a greenhouse. Will stopped the tractor and walked up to Rick.

"Looks like some of the fencing needs repair," he said, pointing down to the south fence.

"Yes, problem is, I have no barbed wire left, used up the rest just last week fixing the north fence," Rick conceded.

"Aren't there some abandoned farms around here?" Will asked, remembering his drive through the valley.

"A couple," Rick started. "Wait, you're not suggesting we go loot one of those farms, are you?"

Will raised his eyebrows. "That is precisely what I'm suggesting. Those owners aren't coming back any time soon, if at all."

Rick agreed reluctantly, and the two decided to head out first thing in the morning, just before dawn. Rick knew of a farm about six miles down the road where the family had left, and there still was a fence up around the property.

*****

By now it was getting dark, so the two men herded the cattle into the barn and drove in the tractor, locked the dead bolt, and headed back to the house, where Kate and Sara had dinner waiting. They had prepared the carrots from the garden and some beans that they had stored in the cellar in the basement. Sara had set the table and poured everyone a glass of water. Kate dished up the carrots and beans, and the four sat there quietly while having dinner. Afterward Sara went down into the basement to listen to music on her iPod, and Kate went up to her bedroom. The two men sat in the living room.

"Be ready about 4:30 a.m.," Rick concluded.

"We better get some sleep," Will said. "Do you want me to sleep downstairs tonight? You have spent the last several days down here."

Rick had put in place another safety precaution that one of the men would sleep downstairs to keep an ear out for anyone coming around the property.

"No, that's OK. I have it handled," Rick answered as he pushed back his recliner.

Will shrugged and headed upstairs. On his way to his room, he saw Kate sitting in her room in the dark, looking out the window.

"Why are you sitting in the dark?" he asked as he entered the room. Kate jumped.

"Oh, you scared the hell out of me! I thought you were Rick," she said with her hand on her heart.

"Rick?" Will asked as Kate got up and closed the curtain.

"He would be upset that the curtain is open, and I might be seen. Rick is very protective of me. Ever since this whole virus started, he has been obsessed about my safety," she answered.

"He worries too much. You can't be seen in the dark." Will opened the window, allowing the breeze to flow in around the curtains.

"That is so nice, the fresh air, and the moon is rising," Kate said, sitting down on the bed. Will sat down beside her.

"I can understand protecting you. I feel the same about my daughter. But he could relax a little," Will contended.

Kate laid her head on his shoulder, surprising Will with the sign of affection. He could feel the warmth of her body close to his. It was almost soothing.

"I knew I would like you," she whispered with a slight laugh.

"Well, I like you too, Kate." He stood and kissed her on the forehead. "And now I must be off to bed. Good night, Kate."

"Good night," she returned.

Will continued down to his room. He sat on the bed, smiled, and thought that having Kate around was good not only for Sara but also for him.

*****

Will woke in the morning, dressed, and headed quietly downstairs so as not to wake Sara and Kate. When he got to the living room, he saw Rick still in the recliner.

"Wake up, Rick. It's already four thirty," he whispered loudly while swatting him with his hat.

"I must have been more tired than I thought," Rick answered as he came to his senses.

The men loaded into Rick's pickup and headed down the driveway. Rick stopped at the gate and opened the padlock, and they proceeded down the road. On the other side of the gate was Will's car. The tires had been removed and the trunk gone through.

"Well, they didn't get any gas. The tank was empty." He snickered.

When they arrived down to the nearest farm, they turned their headlights off and drove slowly down the driveway. At the farmhouse all the lights were off, and there was no sign of anyone. They pulled up alongside the barn, which was large but also falling into disrepair, and the door was already open. Inside it looked as though others had been inside and taken what they needed.

"See what you can find," Rick instructed as they got out of the truck.

The two men looked throughout the barn. Will found some cans of paint, which he loaded in the truck, as well as tipped over buckets and boxes of rusty nails. The whole barn smelled musty. There were no tools left or animal feed, but they did find a stack of two-by-four boards and loaded them into the pickup along with an old gas can. The two men went out to the pasture.

"I will cut the wire, and you can follow behind rolling it up," Rick instructed. The two men worked through the morning rolling up the barbed wire that was still good to use. They loaded it in the truck.

"I think that's about it," Rick said. Will nodded as they both climbed back into the truck and started the engine. Then suddenly they heard a loud bang, and a bullet zipped by the side of the truck. They both turned and looked to see a disheveled old man holding a rifle and taking aim at the truck.

"Give me back my stuff, you bastards!" he screamed and took another shot at them. Rick ducked as the bullet broke the back window. He turned the truck quickly and sped down the driveway. The man shot again as they drove away.

"Holy shit, that was close!" Rick said, looking back, making sure no one was following them.

"A little too close for me," Will said as he took off his coat. Blood was running down the back of his shoulder.

"Crap!" Rick exclaimed and drove as fast as he could to get Will back to the house. When they arrived, he jumped out and helped Will inside, where Kate was waiting for them.

"Just what is going on?" Kate demanded as she noticed the blood on Will's shirt. "Where have you two been?" At that moment Sara came down the stairs and saw Will covered in blood.

"Dad!" she exclaimed before running to open the door to the basement so Rick could get Will down the stairs.

Rick helped Will onto the cot, and Kate cut away his shirt around the bullet wound with a pair of scissors. Will grimaced.

"Sara, look at me," Kate instructed. "Get me clean towels, gauze, and a bottle of water, quickly." Sara went to the cabinet to get the supplies Kate needed, while Kate went to the other cabinet and returned with her surgical kit. Sara brought the items she requested.

"Thank you." She continued. "Now hand Rick a towel. Rick, I want you to hold pressure on his wound to try to control the bleeding until I'm ready." Kate gloved up and prepared a syringe of lidocaine.

"Will, this is only a local anesthetic. I'll get it as deep as I can, but it is not going to take all the pain away. You understand?"

Will nodded yes while Kate grabbed a bottle of rubbing alcohol.

"OK, Rick, release the towel."

Kate cleaned the area around the wound then quickly gave Will two shots of lidocaine, one at the wound site and then one directly inside. Will moaned.

"How are you doing?" Kate asked.

"Hey, piece of cake." Will grimaced as he attempted a smile.

Kate poured water inside the wound and looked and felt for the bullet. Then with a pair of forceps, she proceeded to gently pull out the bullet.

"There!" she exclaimed. "Came out in one swoop!" Kate held up the bullet for Will and the others to see. "No more of these, young man. Next time it might not be so easy." Kate put the bullet down.

"I have no plans," Will laughed, "but I also can't give any guarantees."

Kate looked at the wound again. "I'm not going to sew this up," she continued, "as I do not want to sew up any infection. We'll just have to watch the bleeding." Kate proceeded to cover the wound with gauze as Sara came up and hugged her father.

"Don't worry," he consoled her as he hugged her with his good arm, "I'll be just fine."

Rick sat down in the chair next to the cot and let out a long sigh. "That old man came out of nowhere."

"Where were you, and what were you doing?" Kate demanded again.

Rick stood up. "We were seeing if the farm down the road had any barbed wire so we could repair our fence. I'm going to unload the truck."

Kate finished cleaning up. "Sara, please help me get your father upstairs to his room. He needs rest."

As Kate and Sara helped Will to his feet, he turned and kissed Kate on the cheek. "Thank you."

Kate blushed and smiled. "You're welcome."

CHAPTER FOUR

RICK GOES TO JEFFERSON

IT HAD BEEN ABOUT A month since Will had been shot. He was now pretty much healed up and back at work with Rick in the fields. They had repaired the fence around the farm. Kate was showing Sara how to make jam from the strawberries they had grown in the garden next to the house along with green beans, lettuce, and other vegetables. The family really depended on this garden as a main source of food. Kate knew great care needed to be done to preserve as much of their harvest as possible for the winter months. They also could use some of their harvest for trade knowing that food was in short supply. They were starting to run out of certain things, such as salt, flour, baking powder, and cornmeal, and the biggest item was gasoline for the truck and tractor. Rick had heard that a trading post had been set up in Jefferson by some of the locals.

Rick was planning a trip to see what supplies he could get with the items they had to trade. They had strawberry jam, carrots, eggs, corn, and milk.

"When will we be leaving?" Will asked.

"We?" Rick stated. "I don't think so. I need you to stay here with the women to watch over them."

"I can watch over myself," Kate interjected after overhearing them.

"No offense, Kate," he replied. "I just will feel better with Will here. Besides, he needs to be watching the crops and the cattle. The less you're outside, the safer you are."

"Let me pack you some food for the trip," Kate conceded, "and, Rick, please be careful." The last time Rick had gone to Jefferson, he had taken the truck, but with gas now in short supply and needed for the tractor, he would be going on horseback. One horse to ride, one horse to pack supplies.

"I'll leave in the morning and return in the evening if all goes well. It'll make for a long day, but I don't like being gone too long." He kissed Kate good night and went upstairs early to get some sleep while Kate finished packing up food and some water for his trip. When she finished, she took a box of vegetables down to the root cellar. After some time she heard someone enter the basement.

"Aunt Kate, I came down to get a book to read," Sara said, going over to the bookshelf. Kate watched as Sara carefully picked a book from the collection to read. "Good night, Aunt Kate." Sara said, going back upstairs.

A few minutes later, she again heard someone enter the basement.

"Kate," Will said, "I just wanted you to know that I don't think you can't take care of yourself. But I also care about you and wouldn't want anything to happen to you."

"I understand, Will," she said. "I just don't want to feel like I'm being treated like a child." Kate motioned to Will to come sit down. "I see Sara and wonder, is she like her mother?"

Will shook his head. "No, the opposite. My wife had issues with pain medications, and the last few years had been rough. Sara was often her mother's caregiver. Her mother became very combative, but Sara still insisted on caring for her. Then the virus came. She got ill so fast, and Sara started caring for her mother night and day. I didn't want her to get so close, but I couldn't stop her. Soon her mother passed away. I've thanked God every day since that she's remained healthy."

Kate looked at Will and saw both sorrow and relief in his eyes. She could tell he did not want to talk any more about it. It explained why Will grabbed her hand the other day when she was trying to cut Sara's hair. He was used to protecting Sara from her mother.

"I'll leave you to your work," Will said as he stood up and headed toward the stairs.

"Thank you, Will, for telling me what happened. I am sorry you went through all that pain."

"Thanks, Kate. Good night." Will headed up the stairs. Kate finished in the root cellar and headed upstairs to bed for the night.

*****

Early morning had come, and Rick was already up and getting ready to leave for Jefferson. Kate heard him down in the kitchen, and she went down to help with his supplies for the trip. It was still dark outside and quiet. Rick and Kate did not say a word to each other as they packed up the supplies. When they were finished, Rick turned to Kate. "I will be back as soon as I can," he said, then he left out the back door. There was no goodbye kiss, no "I love you;" he just left. Kate stood there wondering, *Did I do something to upset him? He always kissed me goodbye.* Kate reached for some eggs and a pan to cook them. The sun was just starting to come up, along with a wind blowing the trees outside, brushing them up against the side of the house. Kate took a peek out the curtain of the kitchen window.

"Red sky at morning, sailors take warning."

"So are you a sailor?" Will asked with a laugh, coming into the kitchen.

"Oh, did I say that out loud?" Kate laughed back as she scrambled up some eggs. "Would you like some breakfast?"

"No, thanks. I'm going to get outside. It looks like a storm is heading in, and I want to batten down the hatches," he answered as he put his hat on and headed out the door.

After breakfast Kate proceeded upstairs and dressed in jeans, a button-up men's shirt, a jean jacket, boots, and a stocking cap that covered all her hair. She peeked in at Sara, who was still asleep, then went downstairs and out the kitchen door. She went over to the woodpile and started carrying wood into the house that they would need for the stove. For sure, the electricity would be going out. Will looked up from his work to see her outside. He waved and nodded at her, and she nodded back at him, surprised he did not race over to scold her for being outside. She got back to carrying wood inside till the woodbin was full, by which time Sara had come downstairs. The two smiled at each other.

"Good morning, Sara. Could you help me fill the lanterns with oil today? It looks like there's a storm brewing."

"Sure!" Sara replied. "I hope there is thunder and lightning!"

*****

Rick rode along the gravel road until he reached the main road, unsure how safe it was to travel along the highway. He had his rifle with him, but he also knew his ammunition was in short supply. He would just travel along the side of the road and hope for the best. He felt the wind pick up and saw the clouds rolling in, so he quickened his pace. He just wanted to get to Jefferson and back as soon as possible.

Kate went down to the basement to get the lanterns. They were lined up on the top shelf, so she pulled out the step stool and climbed up to reach the lanterns. Will was on his way down to the basement to get himself a Band-Aid, as he had cut his hand. Kate was on her tiptoes reaching and reaching. The step stool tipped, and just as Kate started to fall backward, Will leaped up behind her and caught her. He set her on her feet and turned her around.

"Holy shit, thank you!" she said. Kate took a step back onto the step stool, making her lips closer to Will's, as she looked into his eyes. She then kissed him, slowly and softly.

"Dad! Aunt Kate!" called Sara, who was just now coming down into the basement. Kate recoiled and looked toward the stairs.

"We are down here," Will called out as Kate returned to reaching up to get the lanterns from the top shelf and Will handing her down a couple.

"Sara, honey, can you grab the oil from the bottom shelf?" Kate asked, stealing a glance at Will. He smiled at her.

"Well, I've got to find that Band-Aid," Will said before removing the first aid kit from the cabinet, applying the Band-Aid, returning the first aid kit, and turning toward the stairs. "And now time to get back outside." Will smiled as he passed by Kate. She did not know what came over her; she thought he just needed to be kissed, and so she did. She smiled to herself.

*****

For several hours already, Rick had been traveling and seen no one along the road. Jefferson was now only about an hour away. The wind had picked up and was colder, and he was hoping he could beat the storm, at least to make it to Jefferson. With Will back at the farm and able to get the animals inside the barn, he knew he could spend the night in Jefferson if he needed. He pulled his collar up against the wind and quickened his horse's pace.

Kate and Sara stayed in the basement and filled the lanterns with oil. They could hear the wind getting stronger outside, and the old house creaked and groaned. When they finished and returned to the kitchen, the sky had become dark with clouds, and the rain began blowing up against the windows. Behind it came the sound of thunder.

"It's coming," Kate said, a moment before the back door blew open. She ran quickly to the door and closed it. "Sara, stay in the house. I'm going outside to help your dad get the livestock in the barn." Kate put on a coat, a hat, and boots and darted outside.

Down in the pasture, Will was trying to round up the cattle. The door to the barn had blown closed; Kate opened it just in time for the cattle to go inside, then closed it again and latched it.

"We need to get the chickens in the coop!" Will shouted through the wind and rain. Kate chased the chickens and shepherded them into the coop. Will grabbed her hand.

"Come on, let's go!" he shouted. The two retreated quickly into the house.

"Wow, that storm came in quick!" Kate remarked, a little shaken, as a clap of thunder rolled through the house. "And it's getting closer." They removed their coats and hats and hung them to dry.

"Yeah. We should get a fire going before it starts getting cold in here," Will agreed, then went over to the woodbin. "Thanks for bringing all this in, Kate. It looks like we will not be getting any more work done today." Will got some of the wood and proceeded to make a fire in the stove. The warmth started radiating through the house.

"Sara, why don't you go down and get a book to read to us here next to the fire?" Kate suggested.

*****

As Rick arrived in Jefferson, the stores and supermarkets along the main street were empty, and the windows and doors were broken out. What resembled a farmers market was set up along the street. People had brought what they thought they could trade. There were some household items, vegetables from farms, chickens, clothing, tools, and canned goods. Money no longer had any value; everything was being done by trade and barter. It was starting to rain, and Rick needed to be quick. People were starting to pack up their items. Soon he was able to barter his eggs and milk for some flour, salt, and baking powder. The jars of jam he traded for vegetable seeds, onions, and cauliflowers.

By this time the rain was really coming down, and most everyone had left. Rick started packing up what he had acquired and started for home. He noticed something left in the road and stopped to pick it up. It was a DVD. It was still in the package, and it was not broken. He tucked it away among his things.

*****

Kate sat down by the fire. "Thanks, Will, for starting the fire. It sure is a cold storm for this late in the spring." Will came and sat down beside her just as Sara was returning from the basement.

"Look," she said, "*A Wrinkle in Time*. I picked it because it starts out with 'It was a dark and stormy night'!"

"Go ahead," Will said. "You want to read it aloud to us?"

Sara started reading. There was a loud crash of thunder. Kate moved closer to Will. The lights went out. Kate got up and lit one of the lanterns, just being able to see from the light of the fire. She sat the lantern next to Sara, and she continued to read. For a couple of hours, they forgot about the storm and Rick being away.

Kate stood up and went to peek out the window. "Wind is sure getting crazy out there."

Will knew Kate was concerned about Rick. "I am sure that Rick found a good place to hunker down for the night."

"Sara, it's getting late," Kate said as the light began to fade outside. "We should be off to bed." Kate offered her hand to help Sara up. The two of them headed upstairs.

"Dad, are you coming to bed?" Sara called back over her shoulder.

"I'm going to tend to the fire here and keep an eye on things. You go up to bed," Will said, putting more wood on the fire. Sara and Kate went to their bedrooms.

*****

Against the wind and the rain, Rick could ride no further. Nearby was a pasture, and out among the pasture next to an old, broken-down truck was a barn. Rick took the horse over to the barn. Inside, it was dry and looked abandoned, as though no one had been inside for quite a while. He found an old lantern hanging on a nail and was able to get it lit. A few feet away was a horse harness hanging on the wall, a couple of pitchforks, some rusted truck parts, and a few sawhorses. Past them, over in the corner of the barn, was something covered by an old, dirty tarp. Pulling it away, he discovered an old buckboard wagon in relatively good shape.

"Now this is a great find!" Rick exclaimed. "Must be what the horse harness is for." Rick examined the wagon. One wheel needed repair, but he found a spare in the back of the wagon. He removed the broken wheel and replaced it with the spare. He checked the brakes and found them to be working. He decided he would hitch up the horses to the wagon in the morning, load it with his supplies, and take the wagon home.

*****

Kate lay in bed listening to the wind and the rain, worried about Rick. Had he decided to take shelter somewhere? He still had not returned home, but it was not unusual for him to get back late. She listened to the rain and the wind until finally she fell asleep.

Will had fallen asleep in front of the woodstove but was awoken by the sound of a loud crash and of shattering glass. Sara ran to the top of the stairs and shouted down to her father.

"Dad, it's Aunt Kate! Come quick!"

Will jumped up and ran up to Kate's room. There, on her bed, he found Kate pinned beneath a large branch from the old oak tree outside her window. It had crashed through the window in the wind. Together, Kate, Sara, and Will lifted the branch until Kate was finally able to crawl out from under.

"Kate, are you all right?" Will asked, helping her to the chair beside the bed.

He could see blood running down her arm to her hand.

She had a large laceration on her forearm. "You're bleeding, Aunt Kate!" Sara yelled.

Will grabbed a pillow and removed the case and wrapped it around Kate's arm. She looked back at the bed where the bulk of the branch had barely missed her. "Looks like I was lucky," she added.

"Sara, can you help Aunt Kate with this cut while I try to clear out this mess?" Will asked, checking again to make sure Kate was all right.

Kate nodded yes and rose to follow Sara down to the basement, where the medical supplies were located.

"Well, Sara, this is a good time to teach you some first aid. So listen to me carefully and follow my instructions, OK?"

"Yes," Sara replied.

Kate grabbed some gauze from the cabinet to help stop the bleeding. "First, we need to try to stop the bleeding as best as we can." She removed the pillowcase Will had tied around her arm and placed the gauze over the cut. Then she went to the other cabinet and returned with a suturing kit and some lidocaine. "Now I need your help in carefully preparing this syringe with the lidocaine to give to me to numb the area, then we can stitch it up. First, you need to wash your hands with soap and water." Sara went over to the sink and washed and dried her hands. "Now put on a pair of gloves. Kate also put on a pair of gloves, and she continued to show Sara how to fill the syringe with the lidocaine. "Now we will rinse the wound with this bottle of water," Kate pointed.

Sara then washed the wound with the bottled water and patted it dry with more gauze. "Thank you. Now I am going to put some lidocaine in my arm to make it numb." Sara watched carefully as Kate injected her arm.

"Did that hurt?" she asked with her eyes wide open.

"A little, but soon I won't be able to feel it at all."

"Now open the suturing kit for me." Sara opened the kit. Kate then threaded her needle driver and started to suture up the wound. Sara never even closed her eyes; she watched with such curiosity.

"Maybe I can be a nurse one day," Sara suggested.

"I will teach you everything I know," Kate answered.

When Kate had finished, they went upstairs to Sara's room. They both lay down on the bed and covered up with the blanket.

"That was scary!" Sara let out before turning and hugging Kate.

"Yes, it was, but you did great," Kate replied. "Thank you for helping me stitch up my arm."

After pulling the branch off the bed and onto the floor, Will went down to the basement and returned with a half sheet of plywood, nails, and a hammer. He covered the broken window then closed the door and went down to peek in Sara's room.

"Is Sara asleep?" he asked Kate, who responded by nodding yes. "How is your arm?" He continued. He took Kate's hand and turned it to see the wound.

"Sara was a good little helper," Kate whispered. "She is quite the little nurse!"

Will smiled and started to head back to his room.

"Will, please don't leave," she persuaded. "Come stay in here with us. It has been a rough night." Will came and lay down next to Kate, with Sara on the other side. "Thank you, Will," she added as she snuggled up close to him. "I am glad you were here."

Will put his arm around her. She sighed. He lay there remembering the kiss from earlier in the day. Was Kate just expressing gratitude? It seemed like much more. Her kiss had passion, which was a little confusing; she was married to his brother. Whatever it meant, he enjoyed it. He closed his eyes and fell asleep.

*****

In the morning the wind and rain had stopped, and the sun was shining. It was quiet in the house until Kate was awoken by the sound of keys opening the door to the house and the sound of someone coming up the stairs. *It must be Rick*, she thought.

"Wow, isn't this a cozy picture?" Rick said sarcastically as he entered the room.

"Rick, you're home!" Kate exclaimed as she got out of bed, climbing over Sara and waking her up. "I was getting worried about you!" She grabbed and hugged him.

"Well, it doesn't look like you're too worried to me," he answered as he gestured at Will. "You all looked pretty cozy."

"Cozy?" Will replied sleepily, yawning.

Kate interrupted, "Hey, what supplies were you able to trade for?" taking Rick's arm and pulling him toward the door.

"Go on downstairs and see, the supplies are on the kitchen table, and take Sara. I want to talk to Will." Kate took Sara's hand and took her down the stairs.

"What's that all about, Aunt Kate?" Sara asked, puzzled.

"Just guy talk, Sara. Let's see what Uncle Rick brought back with him," Kate said, still feeling the tension from upstairs.

Rick stood over Will. "So what went on here last night?" he demanded.

Will stood and motioned for Rick to follow him down the hall. "Did you look in your bedroom?" Will asked. "This is what happened," he said as he opened the bedroom door and showed Rick the plywood covering where the window had been.

Rick entered the room and walked toward the window.

"I haven't had a chance to do anything with the branch just yet," Will added.

"Was Kate in bed when this happened? Is she all right?" Rick walked toward the door. Will stopped him.

"Kate was cut pretty bad, but Sara helped her stitch up her arm. She is fine now," Will explained.

Rick turned to face Will. "But that still doesn't explain why you were sleeping in bed together."

"What was I supposed to do?" Will countered. "Sara and Kate were scared and asked me to stay with them."

"You could have slept on the floor or in the chair," Rick retorted, his voice raising. "Why were you sleeping next to my wife?"

"Son of a bitch, Rick!" Will defended. "What do you think we did? Sara was right there with us."

"Right, so why didn't you sleep next to Sara?" Rick asked, pushing Will.

Downstairs Sara and Kate could hear the two men were arguing.

"Sara, you stay here. I'm going up to see what the ruckus is all about."

As Kate reached the bedroom door, she could hear their conversation.

"Do you want to hear the truth?" Will yelled. "I enjoyed lying next to her, the sweet smell of her hair, the warmth of her body. I could have kissed her—"

Rick punched Will right in the face and knocked him down. Kate swung open the door.

"Stop acting like junior high boys!" she shouted. "Rick, all Will did was exactly what you asked him to do, look out for Sara and I." Kate walked over and stood between Rick and Will. "Now go out and get some work done," she added with fire in her eyes. "I am sure there is some storm damage to deal with!"

"Go ahead, Will," Rick demanded. "Go clean up that bloody nose, and when you're done, go unhitch the buckboard wagon I found and put the horses in the barn. I need to talk with Kate." Will left the room.

"Why did you ask Will to stay with you?" he asked her.

She walked over and sat on the bed. "The branch had come through the window and nearly killed me. I was upset and scared, and so was Sara. You have not even asked me if I am OK." Kate showed Rick her stitches.

Rick took Kate's hand. "Why did you let him lie next to you?" Rick asked.

"You really think we were going to have sex with Sara right there next to us? Get real, Rick!" shouted Kate. "And give me some space! Stop making me feel like a prisoner in my own home!"

Rick was bewildered. "Where is that coming from?" Rick got up and walked to the window. "It's only for your protection. You know that," he reminded her. Kate came up behind Rick.

"Why don't you kiss me anymore?" Rick didn't respond right away. "Oh, why do I care?" Kate lashed out and ran out of the room.

Rick stood there alone in the room, wondering where all her anger was coming from. Had he been ignoring her? He had just been trying to keep them alive and protect Kate. He shook his head and lay down on the bed, just too tired to care.

CHAPTER FIVE

A STRANGER ON THE PROPERTY

IT TOOK A COUPLE OF days to get the damage from the storm repaired, and now everyone was back to their somewhat normal routine. Sara was continuing to learn about the farm. She and Kate were in the vegetable garden. Rick was in the barn mucking the stalls, and Will was finishing some repairs on the greenhouse. All was quiet until Kate and Sara heard the dinner bell ringing down from the barn. They knew it was a warning from Rick that someone was on the property.

Will jumped down from the roof of the greenhouse and grabbed Sara's and Kate's hands and led them to the well pump house to hide. He shut the door and returned to the top of the greenhouse to see if he could see who was coming. He looked down toward the barn, and he could see a man riding up on a horse from the back of their property to Rick, who was standing outside the barn. He could see the man get down from his horse and walk up to Rick.

"My name is Jeff," said the man, sticking his hand out to shake Rick's hand.

"I'm Rick. What can I help you with, Jeff?" Rick asked. He had his shotgun down beside him, leaning against the fence. The man looked pale; his hair and clothes were dirty.

"I am from Jefferson. I used to work at the hospital, and I know your wife, Kate. My son is very sick, and the hospital is now shut down. I was wondering if Kate could come by and check on my son. I know she is a really good nurse." The man's voice was shaky, and he did not look Rick in the eye as he was speaking to him.

Rick explained to the man that Kate had passed away from the virus. He wished him luck in finding another health-care worker in the area and told him that he did not know of anyone still in the valley.

"Oh, then the information I got that someone had seen a woman here at your farm must have been incorrect," the man confessed.

"Yes, it's just me and my brother and his son here now, no women. I sure do miss my wife, and she was a great nurse." Rick did not know if the man was really telling the truth about a sick son, but his senses were telling him that he was lying.

"Well, that is too bad. I am sorry for your loss," the man said, climbing back up on his horse and riding away.

"I wish you luck with your son and hope that he gets well soon," Rick said, walking back toward the barn. Rick watched through the barn door until the man disappeared into the distance.

Will saw the man ride away, and he ran down to the barn to ask Rick what his visit was all about. Kate and Sara sat in the pump house, waiting.

"I wonder what is going on, Aunt Kate," Sara asked. Kate just put her finger up to her lips in attempt to keep Sara quiet.

Will returned with Rick to the pump house and opened the door and let Sara and Kate out.

"We need to get to the house quickly," Rick said, putting his arm around Kate's waist and herding her toward the back porch and into the house.

"Rick, what is going on?" Kate insisted.

Will and Sara followed them into the house, and Will shut the door.

"It looks like having you dress in men's clothes is just not enough. Seems like you were spotted outside," Rick said with concern in his voice.

He told Kate the story the man told him, and Kate said she knew a man named Jeff from the hospital, but he did not have a son.

"That's it. It is decided. You and Sara are to stay in the house for your own safety," Rick demanded.

"Dad! I don't want to always stay in the house!" Sara stomped her feet.

"I have to agree with Sara. We can't stay in the house all the time. Who is going to tend to the garden, milk the cow, pick apples, and hang the laundry?" Kate wondered.

"Let's all calm down for right now and discuss this later. For now, Sara, I need you to stay in the house until we figure this out," Will said to Sara as she responded with a snort, crossing her arms and stomping upstairs.

Kate smiled. "I get her response."

Kate followed Sara upstairs. "Sara, would you like to come with me up to the attic?" she proposed. "I was thinking we might try to find that sewing machine we were talking about."

"Sure!" Sara jumped to her feet. They grabbed a lantern so they could see in the attic. Up on the second floor, the two pulled the cord to lower the pull-down ladder, along with, inadvertently, a bunch of dust.

"Obviously no one has been up here for a while!" Kate exclaimed coughing, then letting out a laugh after she recovered. Kate went up the ladder first and set the lantern on the attic floor next to the entrance. "Come on up, Sara," she invited, extending her hand to help her up the ladder.

Inside, the attic smelled musty. There were boxes, furniture, trunks; everything was covered in dust. After a couple of hard tries, Sara managed to open one of the trunks.

"Look, Aunt Kate, some old clothes and pictures!" Sara held up a photo. "Who is this?"

Kate took the photo from Sara and looked at it. "This is a picture of your aunt Amy," she answered.

"Who's that?" Sara asked.

Kate was not sure if she should tell Sara the story, but she felt the truth is always your best bet. "Rick and Will had a sister—Will's elder sister, Rick's younger. Amy was about thirteen and Will around ten when they went swimming in the river that ran along the back of their property. Their parents had a rule that you could only go swimming if you had someone to go with you. You could not go alone. Amy talked Will into going, but he got bored and wanted to go back to the house. Amy wanted to stay. Will got mad and went back to the house anyway. Later Rick asked Will where Amy was, and he told him she stayed at the river to swim more. Rick ran down to the river to check on her, and he could not find her. The entire family began to look for her. Her body was finally found a couple days later. She had drowned."

Sara took the photo back from Kate. "That's sad. She was pretty. Is that why Uncle Rick is mad at my dad?"

Kate was not sure how to answer the question. "Maybe," she said. "These must be some of her clothes. They look like they might fit you, Sara." Kate held up a pretty pink dress from inside the trunk. "All it needs is a good washing. Let's see what else there might be that fits you."

The two looked through the trunk and found more clothes.

"Look at these hats!" Kate exclaimed, putting one of the fancy ones on her head and another one on Sara. "We can be sophisticated ladies!" They both laughed as they continued through the trunk.

"Hey, what is going on up there?" came a voice from below. The two looked over and saw Will's head popping up from the ladder.

"Hi, Will. We came up here to look for the sewing machine," Kate replied.

"I see it, Aunt Kate. It is over there in the corner." Sara pointed.

Will came up the ladder and went over to the machine and wiped some of the dust from it.

"This was Grandmother's," he reminisced, before something else caught his eye. "Hey, look at this! I remember Grandpa using this old ham radio! I wonder if it still works. Maybe there are others out there communicating."

Kate and Will worked together to get the sewing machine down the ladder, and then Sara handed down the radio.

"Sara, go ahead and bring the clothes and hats from the trunk, please."

A moment later Sara handed down the requested items as well as the lantern.

Will helped Kate move the sewing machine into the living room.

"I'm going to see if I can get this old beast working," she said, examining the machine. Kate sat down at the machine and began to move and slide levers. Will turned to Sara.

"Sara, you want to help me with a project upstairs?"

"Sure, what is it?" she asked. He motioned her to follow as he led her into his room, which was the biggest room upstairs. He went over to the two French doors on the north side of the room.

"See this big balcony?" he asked as he opened the doors. "I want to build a tall wall around the edge of it so that Kate and you can go outside in the sun without being seen." Sara's eyes lit up.

"That's a great idea! Uncle Rick doesn't want us to go outside anymore."

"I know, but let's make this a surprise," he said as he put his fingers to his lips.

Sara made like she locked her mouth with a key and swallowed it, then she smiled.

"I want to paint the inside of the wall." Will continued. "Do you think you can sketch how we can paint it to make it look like the sky, grass, and the sun?" Will handed Sara a pad of paper and a pencil.

"I'll get right on it!" Sara grabbed the pad of paper and darted into her room.

Will went out to the barn to fetch some of the two-inch-by-six-inch boards they had found at the abandoned farm and stack them under the balcony.

"What are you planning, Will?" Rick asked as he walked up behind him.

"Going to fix up . . ." he started to answer. "You know, Rick, you don't need to question everything I do," Will asserted as he stacked more lumber. Rick raised his eyebrows and just walked away.

Rick went into the house, where he found Kate sitting at the old sewing machine.

"Are you trying to fix that old thing?" he asked, somewhat interested.

"Actually, I think I have it already working," Kate responded as she pushed on the pedal. "I oiled the levers, the wheel, and pedal." She pulled on the wheel, and it started turning, and the needle moved up and down. "Oh yeah!" She beamed. "I think with a few more adjustments, I will have her as good as new."

"You know, you are pretty handy around here, Kate," Rick said, giving her a kiss on the top of her head. At that moment Sara came in the room. She had tried on some of the clothes they had found in the old trunk.

"Look, Aunt Kate, these fit!" She twirled around, modeling the shirt and pants.

Rick examined the clothes Sara was modeling. "Are those Amy's old clothes? I recognize that shirt. It was one of her favorites." He looked up at Sara. "Take those off now!" he shouted.

Sara ran out of the room crying. Kate stood up. "Sara, wait!" She turned to Rick. "Sometimes you can be such an asshole!"

Will had heard all the commotion. "What is going on in here?"

"Your daughter is wearing Amy's clothes!" Rick yelled in Will's face.

"Yes, I know that," Will said in return with his hands on his hips.

Rick walked over to the back door. He looked at Will and Kate and then slammed the door as he headed out.

"Will, I'm so sorry. I had no idea that he would respond that way. When I spoke to you about the clothes, you seemed fine with it," Kate said, shaking her head in disappointment.

"I should have known he would react that way. I knew Sara had the clothes, but Rick was very close to Amy. I figured Amy would rather have her niece wear them than sit in a trunk. Where is Sara?" Will asked. Kate pointed up the stairs. Will went up the stairs to Sara's room. She was not there. "Sara!" Will shouted with concern. He began to go room to room, shouting her name. No answer, no Sara. Kate met Will on his way back down the stairs.

"Kate, where is she? She is not anywhere upstairs!" He brushed by her on the stairs and went through out the house, looking and calling for Sara.

Kate started looking in closets and corners, but Sara was nowhere to be found. Will stopped and looked at Kate with a totally panicked look on his face. He turned and ran out the back door.

Rick was in the garden and heard Will shouting Sara's name. He dropped his tools and ran toward Will and grabbed his shoulders.

"Stop! Stop! Quit yelling out Sara's name! Someone might hear you!"

Will pulled away from Rick. "This is your fault! I cannot find her anywhere in the house!" Will started shouting her name again. Rick clamped his hand over Will's mouth.

"Will, stop, someone might hear you. I will help you look for her."

The two men split up and started searching the farm. They looked in the barn, the pump house, the hayloft, and out in the orchard, but no sign of Sara. The two reconnected. "There is no sign of her," Will said in dismay. "This is all your fault, Rick! How could you shout at her that way? She is just a little girl!"

Rick defended himself. "It took me by surprise to see Amy's clothes on her. You know how I feel about our sister."

"Yes, I do, but do not take blaming me for Amy's death out on my daughter!"

"I don't blame you, Will. I did at first, but over the years, I come to understand that you were not responsible for our sister's lack of judgment. I just wished you would have told someone that she was being stubborn and stayed at the river. I know you were just a kid. I am sorry I took it all out on you."

*****

Kate was inside and was thinking, "If I were a scared young lady, where would I hide?"

Kate went down to the basement and went to the armoire. She opened the door and slid open the fake back wall. Inside sat Sara, crying. "Go away! I hate you and Uncle Rick!" Sara turned her face toward the wall.

"I don't like Uncle Rick so well myself right now, but, Sara, we need to try to understand. He loves and misses Aunt Amy, and seeing you in her clothes just reminded him of that. It caught him off guard." Kate climbed in the armoire and sat down. She put her hand on Sara's shoulder. Sara pulled away. They both just sat there quietly for a while. "Sara, I have come to care about you. I know I am not your mother, and I am not trying to replace her. I am just trying to be your friend." Kate tried to reassure Sara to try to gain her trust.

Sara looked over at Kate. "I really don't hate you. I like you, Aunt Kate. You are kind to me." Kate climbed out of the armoire and offered her hand to Sara to help her out. Sara grabbed her hand. "Does Uncle Rick hate me?" Sara asked as she climbed out of the cabinet.

Kate looked Sara in the eyes. "No, sweetie, he doesn't hate you. We could never hate you." Kate hugged Sara. "Let's give Uncle Rick a chance. I am sure he yelled at you just out of surprise to see you in those clothes. Let me talk to him. I know your aunt Amy would be so happy to know that her clothes are being used by such a lovely niece." Sara smiled.

The two went upstairs to the kitchen, and Kate poured Sara a glass of water. Kate stuck her head out the back door and whistled as loud as she could to signal Will. Rick and Will heard Kate's whistle and ran back to the house.

"Did you find her?" Will gasped. Kate stepped aside and motioned toward Sara sitting at the kitchen table. Will ran to her and picked her up to hug her, tears coming down his face.

Rick came in and saw Will hugging Sara and came up to the both of them. "Sara, I owe you an apology." Will sat Sara down, and she went up to Rick. He squatted down to meet her eye to eye. "I am sorry I yelled at you. It's just that you looked so much like my sister, Amy, whom I loved very much. Your dad and I lost her many years ago, and I miss her. Again, Sara, I am sorry."

Sara reached over and put her hand on Rick's shoulder. "I am sorry you miss her. If you don't want me to wear her clothes, I won't."

Rick looked at her and smiled. "No, I want you to wear them. I am sure your aunt Amy would want you to have them." Sara hugged him.

*****

The day had come to an end; everyone was asleep until Rick awoke from the sound of the horses. They were supposed to be in the barn. He ran to the window but could not see anything. He dressed quickly and hurried down the stairs. Will was sleeping on the couch.

"Will, get up," he urged. "Something is disturbing the horses."

Will hopped up, grabbed his pants and boots, and ran outside after Rick but not before Rick grabbed his shotgun. As they approached the barn, Rick gripped his shotgun. The barn door was open.

As they entered the doorway, they could hear footsteps quicken toward them, then something brushed by Rick. Will took off after the shadow and tackled the figure just outside the barn door. Rick pointed the gun at the figure on the ground as Will stood up beside him. They could just see in the moonlight a young man, no more than eighteen or nineteen years old.

"Who are you?" Rick demanded.

"Don't shoot!" the young man pleaded. "I'm from a neighboring farm."

"What the hell are you doing in our barn?" Will inquired.

"Our only horse died," the young man replied, "and I saw that you have three. I was just going to borrow one to plow our fields."

"Borrow?" Rick asked. "It looks more like stealing to me."

"Please," the young man begged, "I'm not armed." He opened his coat to show he had no weapons. Rick lowered his gun.

"Are you alone?"

"Yes," the young man answered.

"Well, you're either really stupid or really brave to come out here alone and unarmed." Will laughed.

"I'm just desperate," interjected the young man.

"I know these are hard times," Rick conceded. "What is your name?"

"Eli Washington," he informed.

"I'm Rick, and this is my brother, Will." The young man nodded.

"Wait a minute, is your father named Chris? Are you from the Washington farm?" Rick asked.

"Yes, do you know my father?" Eli replied.

"Yes, we went to high school together. I thought Chris moved away years ago."

Rick went up to the young man and shook his hand. Eli explained how he and his father moved back recently to the farm. The virus had grown in the city, and it was becoming very dangerous to remain. His grandfather, Wes, was still living and working on the farm, so they packed up and moved.

"Well, I'll be, maybe if you had something to trade, we could spare a horse. I have no issue helping out an old friend. We need as many allies as we can get these days," Rick offered.

"I see you have a cow, but it looks like you don't have a bull. I can trade a bull for one of your horses," the young man offered.

"Bring the bull by this afternoon and we'll see, and ask your father to come. I would love to see him," Rick agreed.

"Thank you," the young man said, reaching out his hand again to shake Rick's. "Thank you so very much. I'll be back this afternoon," he added, then took off down the driveway.

"I don't completely trust him," Rick let out as he watched the young man leave.

"You don't trust anyone." Will smirked.

"Damn straight!" Rick replied.

Will and Rick returned to the house, where Kate and Sara were still asleep, and the sun was just starting to rise. Rick returned to his room and got in bed.

"Is everything OK?" Kate asked.

Rick looked down at Kate. "Yes, everything is fine."

She looked up at him. He leaned down and kissed her, then pulled back and smiled at her. She reached up and lightly traced his face with her fingers. He lay down beside her and pulled her on top of him. She kissed him. She reached down to pull off her nightgown. He grabbed her arms and stopped her. She looked at him, puzzled. "Why did you stop me?"

"I was just thinking how lucky I am to have you in my life. I shudder at the thought of ever losing you," he answered.

"So I am confused. Don't you want me?" She moved off him and lay down on the bed.

"Yes, I do, but I need to get some sleep. Let me just hold you as I fall asleep."

Rick reached over and wrapped his arms around her and closed his eyes. Kate lay there awake, confused by her husband's actions. She still was awake when the sun started to rise.

*****

Will was up and in the kitchen, cooking some eggs.

"What's the matter, Daddy?" Will heard a little voice ask. "I saw you go down to the barn last night."

"Good morning, sunshine," Will replied. "There was a man who just thought he would borrow one of our horses."

"You mean *steal* one of our horses?" Sara corrected. At that point Kate came down the stairs to the kitchen.

"Good morning, Aunt Kate. Did you know a man tried to steal one of our horses last night?"

"No, I did not," she answered, a little taken aback, and turned to look at Will.

"How about I tell you all about it while I finish fixing these eggs?" Will suggested as he continued to prepare breakfast. He filled them in about Eli and the horse and the deal about the bull.

"I'm surprised Rick made such a deal," she responded nervously when Will had concluded. "Well, I guess if they produce the bull, it will allow us to grow our herd." After a pause, she added, "Even though Rick knows the family, Sara, I think you and I should remain in the basement today, just to be safe."

At that time Rick came down the stairs.

"Excellent idea, Kate," he concurred. "We obviously need better security around here. When someone can come onto the property and get in the barn so easily, we are in trouble."

That afternoon Rick was in the barn cleaning horse stalls, and Will was trying to get the ham radio working when he spotted Eli walking a big brown bull up the driveway. An older man was with him. Will called out to Rick to go together to meet them. Rick saw that the man with Eli was his old friend Chris.

"Chris, how the hell are you?" Rick reached out his hand and shook Chris's.

"Rick, you old bastard! Not too well concerning the circumstances," Chris replied.

The two old friends conversed and discussed how the world had pretty much gone crazy. Rick told Chris that Kate had passed away, in attempt to keep his wife a secret.

"We brought the bull as Eli said. Do you have the horse?" Rick motioned for them to follow him to the barn.

Rick entered the barn, went to the stalls, and brought out one of the horses.

"She is a good workhorse and healthy," he said as he presented the horse to Eli. Eli took ahold of the reins and handed Rick the rope attached to the bull. Rick looked over the bull. The bull looked healthy and strong and easy to handle.

"How old is he?" he asked.

"Four years old," Chris replied. The men agreed on the trade.

"It's great to see you, Rick, nice to see a friendly face." Chris smiled.

"Well, if you need anything else, please let us know," Rick offered Eli and Chris as they started to walk the horse back down the driveway. Rick put the bull out in the south field by itself so it could graze.

"Rick, come with me to see if we can get that ham radio working, then we can see if we can reach anyone in the area," Will asked. The two men went back up to the house, where Will had set up the radio in his room. He had found an antenna in the basement and had placed it up on the roof.

"I can't remember what Grandpa did to get this to work, so I'm just going to wing it," Will said as he turned on the radio and spoke into the mic. "Breaker, breaker, this is Camp Campbell. Anybody copy?"

Rick laughed. "What are you, a trucker? And what's Camp Campbell?" Will shrugged his shoulders and repeated himself.

At first all they heard was a lot of static. Then Will just kept trying other frequencies.

"Anybody copy?"

They listened.

"I copy. This is the Hammer, broadcasting from the city of Jefferson. Who is this?"

"This is the Campbells out in Gentry Valley looking to see if anyone was out there." There was silence for a moment.

"I copy that. I am the only one around the area. Nice to hear someone who is nearby."

Rick took the mic from Will.

"Is there any news about our government? Have they found a vaccine? Are the cities safe to return to?" Rick and Will waited for an answer.

"You have a lot of questions. Well, I can only tell you what I have heard from those who have come into Jefferson to trade. There is no vaccine yet, but there are not many women left. Do you know of any women around?" There was a pause. He continued. "As for the government, there is now a curfew under martial law. No one out after dark. Be careful. There are men out there impersonating military looking for anything they can take, including your women." The man laughed. "My advice is if you're in a safe place, stay put and keep your shotgun handy."

Both Will and Rick had a look of disappointment.

"Thanks for the information." Rick handed the mic back to Will.

The radio returned to static. Will turned it off.

"Well, survival is all that matters now, and it will not be an easy effort."

Rick nodded in agreement. "There will be many opportunists and evil people out there that will go crazy under martial law. We need to be ready to defend ourselves."

CHAPTER SIX

KATE'S INFECTION

RICK CAME INTO THE KITCHEN. "Where is Aunt Kate?" he asked Sara.

"She is down in the basement." Sara was in the kitchen peeling and slicing apples.

Rick went down the stairs to the basement and found Kate in the medical cupboard.

"What are you doing?" Rick asked as he approached.

"Nothing," Kate answered as she shut the cupboard door quickly. Rick could see she was trying to hide her arm, the one with the cut from the tree branch.

"Let me see that," he said, trying to grab her arm.

"It's nothing." She pulled her arm away.

"Please, Kate, let me see it. If it is nothing, then there is no harm in showing me."

Kate put out her arm. Rick could see that the cut was red, swollen, and oozing fluid, which were all signs of infection.

"Now that is something, not nothing. How could you let it get like this, Kate?" Rick knew this was a problem.

Kate sat down on the cot. She wanted to save the antibiotics for more serious situations. She had been caring for the wound, but she knew it had become infected. "Well, this looks pretty serious to me." Rick stepped over to Kate and felt her forehead; she was very warm. He went over to the cupboard and looked for a thermometer. He moved items side to side in the cupboard and found the thermometer.

"We need to check your temperature. You feel very warm to the touch."

Kate opened her mouth and Rick stuck in the thermometer. He returned to the cupboard, looking through the shelves, this time looking through bottles of pills for antibiotics.

"Where are some antibiotics?" he asked.

Kate stood up and pulled out a bottle of Augmentin and handed it to Rick and returned to the cot. Rick reached down and pulled out the thermometer.

"It's 102.2. You are running a fever. How many of these are you supposed to take?" he asked, opening the bottle.

"One every six hours should do," Kate replied.

"You're going to need some aspirin for that fever too." Rick grabbed it out of the cupboard.

"I'm going to need some water, Rick," Kate said, taking the medication in her hand. She was reluctant to take them, but she knew at this point she had no choice.

Rick headed back up the stairs to the kitchen, where he got a pitcher for water and a glass. Sara was still at the sink slicing and peeling apples.

"What do you need the pitcher for, Uncle Rick?" Sara asked out of curiosity.

"It's for Aunt Kate," he replied, going back down the stairs, with Sara now following behind.

Rick went to the sink and filled the pitcher and poured Kate a glass of water, and she took the medication.

"Now please lie down and rest."

"I'm fine, and I have things to do," Kate said, standing up.

By this time Will had shown up. "Why is everyone down here?" he asked, walking up to the cot.

"Show him, Kate," Rick directed. Kate showed Will her wound.

"Holy crap, Kate!" Will took ahold of Kate's arm to get a better look at the wound.

"She has a fever of over 102," Rick interjected. "Sara, help Aunt Kate put a new dressing on that, please." Sara ran to the cupboard to get some gauze and then a bowl of warm water and some soap.

Kate lay back down on the cot and sighed, "You win."

Rick and Will went outside back to their chores and left Sara to care for Kate. Sara stayed and helped wash and put a new dressing on Kate's wound.

"Thank you, Sara. I think I will try to get some sleep now. You can go back to working on the apples upstairs. I think I will just sleep right here."

Sara put a blanket on Kate and then went back upstairs, leaving Kate in the quiet. She picked up where she left off with the apples but carefully kept an ear out in case Aunt Kate called for her help.

A couple of hours had gone by, and Sara was finished putting the apples in some jars and was getting ready to take them downstairs to the cellar. Will returned to the house.

"Whoa, pumpkin, let me help you bring those jars downstairs."

Will grabbed some of the jars from Sara, and he went to the basement. They put the apples in the root cellar and then walked over to check on Kate. She was asleep. Will touched her forehead; she was so hot and shivering with chills. Will grabbed the thermometer from off the counter.

"Kate, Kate, I need to take your temperature again." Kate awoke and looked up at Will.

"Why is it so cold in here?" She pulled up the blanket. Sara quickly pulled down the blanket.

"Aunt Kate told me that when someone has a fever, they need to be cooled down. We need to take the blanket off."

Sara gathered up the blanket and threw it on the back on a nearby chair. Will was afraid that Kate's fever had gone up and not down. Kate looked up at Will and opened her mouth so he could place the thermometer under her tongue. Sara and Will waited. Kate's eyes were closed; her skin was pale and clammy. Will reached over and pulled out the thermometer.

"What is it, Dad?" Sara asked nervously.

"It's 104," he answered. "We need to get her in a cool bath to help bring down her temperature. Sara, stay here with her. I need to go get Rick."

Will went upstairs and out the back door; Rick was down at the barn. Rick heard Will come in.

"Will, can you help me with these hay bales?"

"Rick, Kate's fever is up to 104. I need your help," he said, turning back toward the barn door with Rick running after.

"I knew this was going to happen. Kate will take care of everyone else but herself," Rick blamed.

Will stopped in his tracks. "This is not Kate's fault! Besides, it does no good to place blame."

The two men arrived at the house. Sara shouted from upstairs, "I have a cool bath ready for Aunt Kate!"

The upstairs bathroom had a large claw-foot tub. Sara had filled it with cool water about halfway.

The men went down to get Kate. Rick pushed Will out of the way.

"I will carry her upstairs. I don't want you undressing my wife. Sara can help me!"

Rick picked up Kate and took her upstairs to the bathtub. Will followed Rick up the stairs, but Rick shut the bathroom door behind him. Will stood in the hall alone. He could hear Rick asking Sara to help remove Kate's clothes, then the sound of water splashing. Will paced back and forth in front of the bathroom door.

"What can I do to help?" Will asked desperately.

Rick answered, "Go get the pitcher and glass. We need to get her to drink some water."

Will hurried downstairs to get the water pitcher and glass and hurried back upstairs. He stopped in front of the bathroom door and poured the glass full, his hands shaking and spilling water on the floor.

Will knocked on the door. "Here is the water." Sara opened the door, and Will handed her the glass. Sara handed it to Rick. Will came in past the door and stood at the end of the tub.

"Kate, can you please drink some water for me?" He pushed the glass to her lips. She started to drink. She reached up and pushed the glass away.

"I am in pain. My arm is on fire!" she said, grimacing.

"What do you want us to do, Kate?" Will asked, taking her hand.

"Sara, go get me some clean washcloths. Will, if you could get some warm water in a large bowl and add a couple of tablespoons of salt, please." Kate turned to Rick. "If you could just reassure me that everything is going to be OK, that would help me greatly." Kate had tears running down her face. Rick wiped her tears from her cheeks.

"You're going to be just fine. We are going to help you," Rick assured.

Kate smiled and started to shiver again.

"Should we get you out of the bath?" Rick asked, concerned.

"Not yet," she answered.

Rick could see the look of pain on Kate's face. He knew she was a strong woman, and that did provide him with a small amount of comfort but did not take his worry away. Both Sara and Will returned with the items Kate requested.

"OK, now soak a washcloth in the salt water and place it on my arm," she instructed. Will took a washcloth from Sara and did as Kate asked and placed the cloth on her arm.

"Aunt Kate, what is the salt water for?" Sara, always curious, asked.

"It will help draw out the infection. Remember that, Sara. It might come in handy for you someday in the future." Kate tried to smile, but she was feeling dizzy from the fever, and her lips were turning blue.

"I want to get her out of this tub. We can put her on the bed in our bedroom and drape her with a cool, wet sheet."

"Kate, can you stand? I want to get you out of the water."

Rick and Will each put an arm under Kate's on each side of the tub to help her stand. Sara wrapped a towel around her, and Kate stepped out of the tub. Rick then picked her up and took her down to the bedroom and laid her on the bed.

"Will, get a sheet wet and bring it back. Sara, go downstairs and get the thermometer."

Rick went to the dresser and pulled out a nightgown for Kate and helped her put it on. He helped her lie back down on the bed, gently pushed her hair out of her face, and kissed her softly on her lips. "I love you," he remarked. "I will take good care of you."

"I love you too," she said with a smile, then closed her eyes. "I'm so very tired."

Will brought the wet sheet and placed it over Kate, then put a new saltwater washcloth on her wound. Sara came with the thermometer and handed it to Rick. He put the thermometer up to Kate's lips, and she opened her mouth. They all stood there staring at Kate, waiting for the temperature. Will sat down next to the bed and again reached for Kate's hand.

"So is it ready yet?" Sara was anxious.

Rick reached and pulled out the thermometer.

"It's 103. It has gone down. Let's just keep doing what we are doing. It seems to be helping. I am going to get some aspirin and her antibiotic from downstairs."

Rick left the room, and Sara followed after with the water pitcher. "I am going to get Aunt Kate some more drinking water."

Will, alone with Kate, leaned down and kissed her on the cheek.

"You have to get better. I love you, and Sara does too."

Will saw Kate smile. "I love you both too," she whispered.

Sara returned with some water and helped Kate drink. Rick came in with the aspirin and her antibiotics. The three sat there tending to her all day, keeping her cool and changing the saltwater compress on her wound. After many hours Sara had fallen asleep along the bottom edge of the bed. Rick had gone to check on the animals in the barn. Will felt Kate's forehead; she felt cool. He put the thermometer between her lips, and she opened her eyes. He looked at her as he waited, hoping the fever had broken.

"This is when a minute or two seems like an hour," he said with a sigh. Kate giggled.

"Oh, that is encouraging, to hear you laugh." Will removed the thermometer. "It's 101! Now that is much better!" Will had woken up Sara in his excitement.

"Sara, her fever has gone down. I think we are making headway."

At that point Rick walked into the room.

"I don't think she is out of the woods yet. It could just be the aspirin and cool sheets lowering her fever. We need to stay diligent throughout the night. I will take the first watch. You and Sara get some sleep."

Rick sat down next to Kate and motioned Will and Sara to the door.

"I won't be able to sleep." Will stayed in his seat next to Kate.

"Go, Will, and help your daughter get to bed. I am staying with Kate," Rick said, glaring at Will. He reluctantly left the room with Sara.

Rick looked down at Kate; her eyes were open. "Well, you told him, didn't you?" Kate said, smirking at Rick.

"Hey, are you feeling better?" Rick asked, feeling her forehead and then looking at her arm.

"My pain is better, but my head still feels foggy. But yes, a little better." Kate sat up. "Can I get some more water, please?"

Rick filled her glass with water and handed it to her. "Here. Anything else I can get for you? You haven't eaten for quite a while. How about something simple like some scrambled eggs?"

"I guess I should try. Don't have much of an appetite." Kate put her hand to her stomach.

"I will be right back, but please lie back while I am gone. You still look pretty pale." He helped Kate lie back and left the room, leaving the door open.

Will had been sitting in a chair at the end of the hall in the dark. When he saw Rick go downstairs, he went to Kate's room. He walked into her room quietly and sat down in the chair next to the bed. Will looked at Kate. He had developed strong feelings for her and not the type that you have for your sister-in-law. He loved her soul-soothing laugh, her smile, the sound of her voice. His world had been dark, but now with her, he could see light. Being around her was like coming home, a comfort, peace. These feelings made him feel good but also made him feel guilty; this woman belonged to his brother. He touched her cheek; Kate opened her eyes. She looked up at Will and returned his touch by placing her hand on his chest. He covered her hand with his. She could feel his heart beating.

"Thank you," she said.

"For what?" he asked.

"For helping to care for me, for just being here," she answered.

"I wouldn't be anywhere else," he returned.

Rick entered the room, and Kate pulled her hand away from Will.

"What are you doing in here? I'm not ready for you to take over yet," Rick scolded as he brought over the scrambled eggs to Kate.

"I was going back to my room and saw her in here alone. I was just checking on her. I'll go." Will left the room, turning back toward Kate as he shut the door.

Kate sat up, and Rick set the tray of eggs on her lap. "Thank you, Rick."

"You're welcome. I am going to go down and check the doors. I thought I heard some movement outside while I was in the kitchen."

Again, Rick left the room. Kate slowly started to eat the eggs he brought. She could hear Rick downstairs talking to himself out loud. She chuckled. He had always done that from the first day they were married. She finished the eggs and placed the tray beside the bed. She yawned and lay back down and closed her eyes. When Rick returned, she was asleep. He put a light blanket over her and just stood there for a moment, watching over her as she slept. He felt both anger and compassion for her, anger because he felt she did not take care of herself, and this would not have happened if she had. But he had compassion; he did not like to see her suffer or be in pain. He lay down next to her on the bed. It had been a long couple of days.

*****

He woke in the morning, and Kate was sitting in the chair beside the bed, looking over at him.

"Kate, you are up." Rick got out of bed and went over to her and felt her forehead.

"I'm pretty sure my fever has broken, and my wound looks much better. If you would help me, I would love to go downstairs and join the land of the living," she suggested.

He helped her with her robe and slippers and then escorted her down the stairs and into the kitchen. Kate sat at the kitchen table.

"Do we have any tea left?" she asked. Rick went to the cupboard to look and pulled out a box of peppermint tea.

"It looks like it's still good," Rick said, looking at the box. "I will make you some."

Rick filled the kettle with water and put it on the stove. He came and sat down next to her at the table.

"It seems that Will has become very fond of you," he mentioned.

"Yes, is that a problem? I would think you would want us to get along," Kate countered.

"Yes, I do, so you like him too?" he reacted.

"I like both Will and Sara. They are family," she acknowledged.

Rick stood and went over to the counter and put a tea bag in a mug. The kettle started to whistle.

"Aunt Kate, you're up!" Sara shouted as she came down the stairs. She ran up and hugged Kate from behind.

"I am feeling much better." She grinned.

"I am so glad!" Sara beamed.

She went to the bread box and pulled out a loaf of bread and started to slice a piece for everyone. Rick brought Kate her tea and then got some jam to go with Sara's slices of bread. They all sat down at the kitchen table. At that point Will came down and joined the family at the table. He sat next to Kate and wrapped his arm around her shoulders.

"I am so happy that you are feeling better. You scared me there for a while."

"I scared myself," she noted while sipping her tea.

"Let's put this whole thing behind us. Will, we have work to catch up on." Rick went toward the back door. "You, my dear," he said, pointing at Kate, "your job is to rest today and take care of yourself."

He opened the door and went out the back. He stopped a moment on the porch, then went toward the barn with tears in his eyes; they were tears of relief.

Will instructed Sara that her job for the day was to make sure Kate would take it easy and to help her with anything she asked. "So I don't want to hear that she has done too much today."

"I am on it, Dad. You can count on me."

CHAPTER SEVEN

THE BALCONY

WARM SPRING DAYS HAD TURNED into hot summer ones. Will was finally finished building the privacy fence on the balcony. It took a while since he was trying to keep it a secret. Sara had completed her design to be painted on it. It had green grass all around the bottom and blue sky around the top.

"I wanted to add a bright yellow sun, some pretty pink flowers, and some butterflies fluttering back and forth. So I made them out of the paper you gave me and some markers and scissors I found in the kitchen," Sara said, displaying her work.

"This looks great!" Will exclaimed. "This will be perfect for the green and blue paint I brought up from the barn. And I love your cutouts."

"Remember, though," Will warned as he opened the doors to the balcony to show Sara what he had built, "be really quiet. We still want this to be a surprise."

Sara agreed and stepped out onto the balcony into the bright sun. Will handed her a can of green paint and a brush to start adding the grass along the bottom of the fence while he added the sky with the blue paint.

When they finished, Will brought up some plants that he had potted and lined the balcony with them. He also brought out a small table and a couple of chairs that he had found in the attic. Sara found a tablecloth in the linen closet and put it over the table. They both stood back and admired their work.

Back inside, she exclaimed, "Aunt Kate will love it!"

"Go get ready, and then get Kate," Will responded. "I have a few finishing touches I want to do."

Sara left to get ready for the balcony unveiling.

She went running into her room and got the pink dress they found in the attic, which Kate had repaired and fixed up. She put the dress on and looked at herself in the mirror. She put on a pair of shoes that they also found in the attic, then brushed and fixed her hair with a pretty pink ribbon Kate had given her to match the dress.

"Perfect," she said.

Will had gone down to the kitchen and cut up some apples and peaches and placed them on a plate and brought them out to the little table on the balcony. Sara went down to the basement to get Kate.

"Aunt Kate," Sara said excitedly, "I need you to go put on your prettiest dress and fix yourself up and come to Dad's room!"

Kate gave Sara a puzzled look and thought, *What an odd request.*

"OK, I'm not sure what you have up your sleeve, but I'll go along with it." Kate smiled. She went up to her room and to her closet and pulled out her favorite dress. It was green, so it matched her eyes. She put the dress on and went over to the mirror.

"Wow, I need to do something with this hair!" she said to herself.

She went over to the dresser, picked up her hairbrush and a pretty barrette, and fixed her hair, then put a little lipstick on her lips and a dab of perfume on her neck. She slipped on a pair of heels and looked in the mirror.

"Look at that. There is a woman looking back." She laughed. "I haven't seen one of those for a while."

She then turned around and headed for Will's room. When she arrived, both Will and Sara were standing near the closed doors to the balcony, both trying hard to contain their excitement.

"Wow, Aunt Kate, you look beautiful!" Sara exclaimed as she ran up and grabbed her hand.

"You look pretty as well, Sara," Kate replied.

Will looked over at Kate. Her green dress highlighted her eyes, her red lips looked kissable, and she smelled like sweet vanilla.

"You both look wonderful," Will beamed. "Kate, are you ready for your surprise?"

Kate's heart was pounding. "Sure! I have no idea what it is, but I can't wait to see it!"

Will opened the doors. Kate walked forward and out into the sun and onto the balcony, her eyes widening as she saw the painting along the fence.

Kate walked around the balcony, smiling and looking at all the plants and the little table with chairs. She turned her face up to the sun and closed her eyes. How warm and bright the sun was on her face! She now had a place to go outside undetected and feel the sun on her skin, smell the fresh air, and feel the wind blow through her hair.

Kate looked over at Will with joy in her eyes and mouthed, "Thank you." He smiled at her.

"You're welcome," he whispered.

Kate looked at Sara and put her hand to her heart. "I love it!"

Sara grabbed Kate's hand and brought her to the table. Will came over, pulled out Kate's chair and motioned for her to sit down, and then did the same for Sara. He then proceeded to pull out the two fancy hats they found in the attic and handed them to the two beautiful ladies to wear. Kate stifled a laugh and smiled. "Now we can be sophisticated ladies." The two ladies put on their hats and posed as though they were getting their picture taken, then proceeded to have their provided delicious snack.

Rick walked out onto the balcony. Kate looked up at him; she wasn't sure how he was going to react to the balcony. He looked at her and smiled, and she smiled back. He walked around the balcony, looking at Will and Sara's handiwork. Sara and Kate gathered up the dishes to take down to the kitchen.

"It looks great!" Rick said.

"So you approve?" Will asked.

"Approve? Why didn't you tell me about it?" Rick said, smiling and patting Will on the back. "I would have helped!"

Will sat down at the little table, puzzled. He never knew how Rick was going to react to anything.

Rick went down to the kitchen and hugged Kate.

"You look so very pretty, and I totally approve of the balcony."

"It's beautiful, isn't it?" Kate agreed. "Now I should go change and get some dinner prepared."

Kate started for the stairs, but Rick grabbed her. "No, wear the dress. You look so nice." As he kissed her quickly, he said, "But as for me, I am a dirty mess." Rick headed upstairs to clean up for dinner.

"Wow, Aunt Kate," Sara remarked, "seeing you in that pretty dress all fixed has put Uncle Rick in a very good mood!" Kate smiled at Sara.

"Maybe it has," she answered.

After finishing preparing dinner and setting the table, they all sat down together. Kate and Sara had made some stew of potatoes, carrots, and onions from their garden and some beef fat Kate had saved. But the treat for the night was some biscuits they were able to bake with the goods Rick was able to obtain in Jefferson and some strawberry jam Sara and Kate had made.

"Thanks for the good eats, Lord. Amen," Will prayed, smiling.

They all ate and talked and laughed. Sara was watching both her dad and Uncle Rick; they both were not just looking at Aunt Kate but also staring. They were both smiling at her and talking and laughing, which they both usually did, but this was different.

After dinner Will helped Sara clear the table.

"Dad," Sara asked, "why were you looking at Aunt Kate in that way?"

"I'm not sure what you mean, pumpkin," Will said, genuinely confused by her question.

"You know," Sara pushed, "you looked at her like a woman instead of as Aunt Kate."

Will motioned for Sara to sit down at the table with him. "Kate is a woman, yes, but I think I understand what you mean. She is not only my sister-in-law but also my friend, and I'm glad she's in our lives," he attempted, not sure what else to say, knowing Sara meant something more, that he had been flirting with Kate and had been caught.

"I understand." Sara laughed, then proceeded into the kitchen to help Kate finish with the dishes.

Will rejoined Rick in the living room to discuss their plans for tomorrow.

"We're going to need to cut the hay in the field before it rains," Rick stated.

"Yeah, we do," Will concurred. "Let's get an early start before it gets too hot." Will stood. "Do you want me to take watch downstairs tonight?" he asked, though he already knew the response. He just could not understand why a man who had someone warm and soft to sleep with would opt for sleeping downstairs more often than not.

"No, I'll stay down here tonight," Rick answered.

He shook his head and went up the stairs, pausing at the top when he heard Kate come up to Rick.

"Are you coming up to bed?" she asked.

"No, I'm doing the watch tonight," he answered.

"OK, how about I go get a book to read and join you? Maybe we could sit on the couch together for a while," she suggested.

"Sure," Rick said.

Kate hurried up the stairs. Will had just gotten into his room as she came by; she had not seen him. She went into her room, stopping first at her mirror to fix her hair and put a little more lipstick on as well as add some blush to her cheeks before slipping out of her dress and into a satin nightgown. She felt the softness of the satin on her skin. She took a deep breath, then started for the stairs, full of anticipation.

Will came out of his room just as Kate reached the bottom of the stairs; he stopped at the top to watch and listen.

Rick was fast asleep in the recliner. Kate walked up to him, took the book from his hands, and laid it down on the table beside him and then covered him with a blanket. Will could hear her sigh. She stood there and just looked at Rick for a while, then turned to come up the stairs, tears in her eyes.

When she was halfway up the stairs, she noticed Will. He reached out his hand to her, which she accepted. He led her up the stairs and down the hall to his room, shutting the door behind them before sitting her down on the bed. He stood in front of her, wiping the tears from her cheeks before sitting down beside her on the bed. Kate leaned in and put her head on his shoulder; Will responded by putting his arm around her waist and drawing her closer to him. He reached down for her chin and pulled her face up so he could look into her eyes, which were full of disappointment. He leaned over and kissed her softly on the lips, tasting the saltiness of her tears. She returned the kiss. He gently laid her down on the bed and kissed her again. She looked up at him and brushed the hair out of his face with her fingers and smiled at him. She reached up and felt his chest, then pulled him down to her and kissed him again. She felt the pressure of his body against her and sighed at the pleasure. He began to kiss her down to her neck, sending a warmth throughout her body she had not felt in a long time. She moved her hands down his body, feeling his muscles and his strength. She felt him slide his hand across her thigh and up to her breast. Her breathing quickened, and her heart raced. She knew in her mind it was wrong, but her body disagreed. He gently caressed her breast. She let out a soft moan.

Kate knew if she did not stop this now, things would go too far. She was torn between pleasure and guilt. She pushed and guided him down on the bed and propped herself on top of him. She reached down and removed her gown, leaving herself naked. He sat up with her on his lap and took her breast in his mouth. She slid him inside her and put her body in motion, satisfying her desire along with his. She felt the warmth and strength of his body, which was so comforting. She lay down beside him and put her head on his chest.

"Thank you, Will," she said softly.

"I should be thanking you." He smiled.

The two lay there in the quiet of the night and drifted off to sleep.

Will woke in the morning with the sun shining through the window. Beside him, his bed was empty; Kate had left sometime during the night. He got up and dressed and went down to the kitchen. Kate was in the kitchen, and Rick was still asleep in his recliner.

"Good morning," Will said as he dared a kiss on Kate's cheek. She blushed.

"Good morning," she returned.

In the living room, Rick stirred.

"I hate it when I fall asleep in my recliner," he complained, rubbing his neck as he rose and came into the kitchen.

"Good morning. Did you sleep well, Kate?" he asked.

"Best night's sleep I've had in a long time," she replied. Rick just looked at her.

"Why is that?" he asked.

"I guess I was just tired," she answered as Will smiled from behind Rick.

"Well, we need to go ahead and get that hay cut before it gets hot out," Will interjected as he grabbed his hat and headed out the kitchen door.

Rick went upstairs to change. Kate sat down at the kitchen table, remembering the night with both pleasure and a little guilt.

CHAPTER EIGHT

KEN AND JOHN

IT TOOK A COUPLE OF days, but Will and Rick finally got all the hay cut and baled. They were putting up their tools for the day when they heard a couple of horses coming up the driveway. Will ran to the dinner bell and rang it a couple of times, warning Kate they had company. She and Sara were already downstairs and heard the bell, so Kate walked over and locked the basement door. Kate came over to Sara, sat down beside her, and put her fingers to her lips.

Will met up with Rick, who was holding a shotgun, in the driveway as the men arrived.

The two men were on horseback. One of them was a heavy man with a mustache wearing a cowboy hat. The other man was thin, clean-shaven, and dressed in jeans and a T-shirt. He was younger than the man with the hat. Both of the men were wearing a sidearm.

"Can we help you?" Rick asked.

"Good afternoon," one of the men answered as he tipped his hat. "We just moved into the farmhouse down the road about five miles from here. "I'm John, and this is my son, Ken." John motioned over to the thin man.

"I'm Rick, and this is my brother, Will. We were down at that farm a couple months ago and saw only an old man."

"We just got there a few days ago and found it empty. We came from Des Moines. We've been looking for a safe place. The city is getting crazy, and the virus is spreading. We wanted to come by and introduce ourselves and see if you had any work we could do in exchange for some food, and my wife said it would be the neighborly thing to do."

"Wife?" Rick responded, puzzled. "You're a lucky man if your wife is still with you."

"Yes, I am," John responded, glancing around the farm. "Is your wife around? My wife would love to meet her. There's just not many women left."

"That's true," Rick conceded. "There aren't any women around here as far as I know. I'm not as lucky as you. My wife passed toward the beginning of the pandemic."

"Sorry to hear that, Rick," John said. "Can we bother you for a drink of water? It's a hot one today." John and Ken got down from their horses.

"Sure," Rick replied before looking at Will and motioning him toward the house. "Will, could you go get a pitcher of water and some glasses?"

Will went into the house and directly down to the basement.

"Kate, it's me, Will," he whispered as he tapped on the basement door. She opened the door. "Kate, you and Sara should go get in the armoire."

"Is there trouble?" she whispered.

"Might be," Will answered. He shut the basement door and went up, then opened the cabinet to get a pitcher. He filled the pitcher with water and grabbed some glasses.

When he arrived back outside, the men were all sitting on the front porch. Will poured each man a glass of water.

"This is a nice farm you got here," Ken remarked.

"It has been in our family for three generations," Will replied.

"So would you happen to have any work that we could do in exchange for some food?" John asked again.

"Sorry, no, maybe another time," Rick interjected. "We just finished bringing in the hay, and we're needing a bath."

"Yes, it has been a long day," Will added with a smile.

Rick noticed John trying to see through the window.

"You sure have your place all closed up," John said.

"Yes, we try to keep the curtains closed to help keep the house cool with all this heat," Rick replied, feeling uneasy with all these questions about the house. "So you said you been here for a couple weeks?" he asked to change the conversation.

"Yep, it looks like you're doing well," John said, then pointed out to the fields.

"We have been lucky," Rick replied.

"And hardworking." Will laughed. "And I hate to be unneighborly, but I would really like to get that bath," Will added, smelling his armpits. The men laughed.

"We understand," John said. "It was nice to meet you. Maybe we can drop in another time and see if you have any work."

The two men got up on their horses and rode off down the driveway. Rick looked over at Will.

"I don't like this at all," Rick declared as he and Will watched the two men until they were out of sight. "I think we should keep the ladies down in the basement for a while. I have a feeling they're going to be back." Rick stepped off the porch to get a better look down the driveway.

"Why?" Will asked. "Do you think they don't believe us?"

"They wanted to see the inside of the house and were trying to look through the windows," Rick replied. "No, I don't think they were satisfied at all with our answers." Rick went back inside the house, and Will followed. They both knew they needed to come up with a plan.

They went down to tell Kate what had happened, and she agreed it sounded suspicious.

"I have an idea," Rick interjected. "I will go down to the old Gentry farm tomorrow. I'll ride down there and check out their story. I can say I'm just stopping by to see how they are getting along and if they need anything. I can see if they really are staying there and if John really has a wife."

"Sounds like a good idea," Will agreed. "I'll come with you."

"I think it's best if you stay here with the girls. Not that Kate is not capable of taking care of herself," Rick explained, smiling at Kate, "but that we need eyes on the outside of the house."

Will agreed, and they set their plans for Rick to go down to the old Gentry farm in the morning.

*****

Rick had gone back down to the barn to finish putting the day's tools away and to put the animals in the barn. Will came down to help. The men put the animals in the barn and were feeding the horse.

"Rick, can I ask why you and Kate never had any children?" Will asked out of the blue.

"That really isn't any of your business." Rick didn't even look up, he just continued with the horses. "And why so curious now?"

"Kate has been so good with Sara. I just thought she would have been a great mother."

Rick looked up at Will. "Kate is a nurse and has cared for many people."

"Yes, that is true, but caring and loving a child is different. Never mind. I do not want to pry." Will could see that he had touched on a subject that Rick did not want to share. He started to the barn door.

"Wait, Will!" Rick stopped him. "Kate and I wanted to have children, and we tried. We went to a specialist to see what the problem was and why she was not conceiving. They ran a battery of tests on Kate, but nothing seemed to be wrong. They then, of course, turned to me. My test determined that I could not give her a child. That was a difficult time for me, being unable to give her a child of our own. We discussed the options like adoption or donor sperm but decided if we could not have a child of our own, it just was not meant to be. It was a hard choice, but I feel that we made the right choice for us. Besides, I don't think I would have had the patience to be a father." Rick smirked.

"Ha, yes, patience is not your best virtue." Will laughed. "I am sorry, Rick, but now you have a niece, and I need all the help I can get to keep her safe."

The brothers finished up outside and went back to the house.

*****

First thing the next morning, Rick and Kate were up, and Sara followed Will down the stairs.

"Rick, I don't like the idea of you going down to check on those men by yourself," Kate stated with concern.

"I understand, but I need Will here to keep an eye out," Rick replied. "That is very important to me."

"Well, that doesn't make me feel any better," Kate added.

"It doesn't make me feel better either, but we have to think about what is best."

Kate looked over at Rick, who grinned just before getting up from the table and heading out to the barn. Will followed after him.

"Be careful, brother. Do you have your gun?" he asked.

"Yes."

The two men got quiet as Rick finished saddling up the horse. He climbed up into the saddle, nodded at Will, and rode away.

Will went up to the vegetable garden on the back side of the house. Kate and Sara were inside canning fruits, occupied not just by the activity at hand but also by their silent thoughts of Rick and the prayers each one clung to for him to return unharmed.

*****

The morning had been long and quiet, and Rick still had not returned. Will had finished in the garden and had come in for a drink of water.

"It's a warm one again today," he said as he poured himself the last of the water in the pitcher.

"Could you go down and get us some more peaches, please?" Kate asked.

"Sure."

Will went off down to the orchard. A moment later Kate heard the side door open.

"Wow, you're pretty fast there, mister," Kate said as footsteps came toward the kitchen.

"Not fast enough," said a man holding a knife. It was Ken, the man who came with his father yesterday.

Kate pushed Sara behind her.

"Well, it looks like your hubby was lying," Ken said, laughing. "Not only does he have a wife but also a daughter—double the jackpot!" Ken came closer. "What might your name be?"

Kate backed up further, pushing Sara toward the back door.

"My name is Kate. What can I do for you?" she asked, shaking.

"Well, that should be obvious," Ken said as he licked his lips. "You and her are coming back with me."

"And why would we do that?" Kate asked as she stepped back and pushed Sara even closer to the back door. Ken reached out and grabbed Kate's arm.

"You need to hold it right there!" Ken said. "I have plans for you and for the girl. First, I will have my way with you, then let my friends do nasty things to you, and then trade your services for goods like gas and food." Kate pushed back and knocked Sara toward the back door.

"Sara, run!" Kate yelled. Sara opened the back door and ran as fast as she could to the orchard. Ken turned Kate around and pulled her toward the door and slammed it shut.

"That was not very smart," he said, pulling her. Kate pulled back, but Ken dragged her back to him and held the knife to her throat. "You wouldn't want me to hurt you now, would you?" Ken said, cutting her face slightly.

Kate stopped pulling. "OK, let's just go. Let's just leave my daughter here," Kate said, hoping to persuade Ken to just leave with her and not Sara. "Let's just sneak out the door," she said, indicating the back door, knowing Ken would probably refuse and want to go out the front. One of Rick's shotguns was always beside the front door.

"No," Ken said, "we will do this my way and go out the front door." Ken had Kate walk in front of him, keeping the knife to her back. As they got closer to the front door, all Kate could think about was grabbing the shotgun.

Sara had almost reached the orchard when Will saw her running toward him. He dropped the peaches.

"Dad, he's got Aunt Kate!" she cried, out of breath.

"Who's got Kate?" Will grabbed Sara's shoulders.

"Some man who just came into the house," she replied.

Will told Sara to hide in the pump house and began running toward the house. He heard a gunshot blast.

Inside the house, Kate had reached the front door and lunged for and grabbed the shotgun, barely turning around to take aim, and shot the intruder. Will ran inside, where he saw Kate holding the shotgun and Ken dead on the floor.

"Oh my god! Kate, are you all right?" She nodded, paralyzed. Will looked down at the dead man.

"That is one of the men from yesterday."

Kate was still standing there holding the shotgun.

"Here, Kate, give me the gun," Will said as he walked up to her slowly and took the gun gently from her hands. Will set the gun down; Kate burst out crying and fell into Will's arms.

"You're shaking," Will said. "Come sit down." Will had Kate sit down at the kitchen table. "Are you hurt?" he asked.

"I don't think so," Kate said as her crying subsided, and she touched the small cut on her face, still covered in the man's blood from the shotgun blast.

Sara came in the back door; she stared at the blood all over Aunt Kate.

"Sara, go upstairs now!" her father demanded.

"What happened? Is Aunt Kate all right?" Sara started walking toward Kate.

"Sara, upstairs now!" Will demanded again. Sara turned and stomped up the stairs.

Will went back to the body; he grabbed a blanket from the couch in the living room and wrapped the body up in it. Just then Rick came through the back door.

"Hello." Rick stopped, seeing Kate covered in blood. "Oh my god! Are you all right? What the hell happened?"

"I shot him," Kate said softly.

"You did what!" Rick yelled. Will came into the kitchen.

"Rick, I could use your help, please," Will said. Rick went with Will back into the living room.

"What the hell happened here? Is Kate OK?" Rick looked down at the body wrapped in a blanket. Will pulled back the blanket to show Rick the man's face.

"That's Ken, one of the men here yesterday. No wonder no one was at the Gentry farm," Rick said. "Where is John?"

"It looks like this one came alone," Will said, looking down at Ken. "But right now we need to clean up this mess before his father shows up."

"Did he hurt her? He better not have fucking touched her," Rick desperately asked.

"I'm not sure what happened. I'll start cleaning up. I think you should go help Kate and make sure she is OK," Will suggested.

Rick stood there for a moment, composing himself before going into the kitchen. Sara had come back down the stairs and was standing next to Kate.

"Aunt Kate, are you OK? What did you do to that man?" Sara said, helping Kate wipe off her face and hands.

"Sara, how about we help Aunt Kate get out of those clothes and into a bath?" Rick said as he walked over to Kate.

"I am capable, Rick," Kate snapped as she stood up. Then she recovered herself. "I'm sorry, but it's not every day that I shoot someone." She turned to climb the stairs.

"Should I go up and help her, Uncle Rick? What happened?" Sara asked.

"I think it's better to leave her alone for right now," Rick said. "Why don't you go upstairs and keep an ear out if Kate asks for help? Your dad can fill you in later."

"OK, I'll do that," Sara said as she proceeded back up the stairs.

Will had gone out and got a bucket of water and some old towels and started cleaning up the blood on the floor and walls. Rick joined him.

"You know that his father is going to come looking for him," Will said, concerned.

"You know the river out behind our property?" Rick asked. "We can dump the body there, and no one will know."

"That is a good idea," Will agreed.

"I'll get the horse ready," Rick said, "and I can take the body out just after dark."

"I'll take it. You need to stay here with Kate. Been a hell of a day for her. She needs you."

Rick agreed. Will finished cleaning and went down and saddled up one horse and tied the body to the other horse. Soon as it was dark, Will rode off to dump the body. When he returned, he put the horses in the barn and returned to the house. It was quiet. He went upstairs and saw Kate and Rick in their room.

"Everything is taken care of, Rick." Will stopped to let him know. "I will stay downstairs tonight to keep an eye on things." Rick nodded; Kate smiled. Will proceeded down to Sara's room. She was in bed but not asleep.

"Sara, how come you're not asleep?" he said, tucking her in bed.

"No one will tell me what happened. What happened, Dad?" Sara untucked herself and sat up in bed. Will had decided to tell Sara the truth and explained what happened. "Dad, Aunt Kate kept pushing me toward the door. Then told me to run." Sara's eyes widened.

"You did the right thing coming to get me. Kate was pushing you, trying to keep you safe, and for that I am very grateful because here you sit." Will hugged Sara.

"She takes good care of me. I think I might love her," Sara said, lying back down in bed.

"Me too, sweetie. Now try to get some sleep. I am going to be downstairs if you need me." Sara smiled and closed her eyes.

Will went downstairs and checked to make sure all the doors and windows were locked and then stretched out on the couch in the living room. He lay there in the quiet listening; soon he fell asleep.

*****

He was awoken early in the morning by a loud knock on the front door. Will went to the entryway window and peeked through the curtain. It was John, the father of Ken, who now was floating in the river. John knocked again. "Just a minute," Will said. He quickly went to the stairs to warn Kate and Rick, but Rick was already down the stairs; he had also heard the knock at the door.

"I have Kate and Sara locked in the bathroom upstairs."

"It's John," Will informed. "I think only one of us should go answer the door."

Rick nodded in agreement as he went into the kitchen, where he could listen and be nearby.

"Who's there?" Will asked as he approached the front door.

"It's John. I came by yesterday with my son, Ken. I am looking for him. Have you seen him?"

Will unlocked the door and opened it. "No, John, I have not seen him. What's going on?" Will said with as much concern in his voice as he could manage.

John explained that Ken had left yesterday to look for some work around the valley, but he never returned.

"I found his horse tied to your gate. You sure you haven't seen him?" John asked, stepping closer to Will, trying to see inside the house.

At that time Rick came around the corner of the kitchen. "Hey, John! Come on in." Rick gestured for John to come in and led him to the living room. "Please sit down. What can we do for you?"

"As I was telling Will, my son, Ken, is missing, and I found his horse tied to your gate. Have you seen him? He must be around here somewhere." Will was trying to think quick on his feet for an answer.

"Only person we seen was a fella that rode through here on a horse yesterday. He was also looking for food and work. Seems a lot of people are heading out here to get away from the city."

"He was not a pleasant man, seemed a little desperate," Rick added. "I can saddle up and help you look for him. I can see you're pretty concerned."

"No, but if you see him, please tell him I'm looking for him. He just might have found some work." John stood and shook Rick's hand and headed for the door.

Will opened the door for John. "Hope you find him soon." John nodded as he returned his hat to his head and stepped outside.

Will shut and locked the door as he and Rick watched out the window as John walked back down the driveway.

"Now he doesn't have a horse, and when they came by, they did have horses. But now he is saying Ken's horse was tied to our gate." Will looked puzzled.

"We are going to have to be more diligent in securing the farm and about protecting Kate and Sara. More people are coming here from the city looking for food and shelter, and it is getting more dangerous."

Will nodded. "I hear you, brother. You were in the military. What ideas would you have to secure our home, crops, and livestock?"

"We could start with more fencing around the immediate area of the house and backyard garden and topping it with some barbed wire," Rick suggested.

The two men decided that in the morning, they would start work on securing the farm, starting with more fencing. Rick headed upstairs, and Will bedded back down on the couch. He lay there with his eyes wide open. "Now I will never get back to sleep."

Rick went back upstairs and let Kate and Sara out of the bathroom. "It was John, Ken's father, but we set him off the path, and he left." Kate was shaking, so Rick wrapped his arm around her waist. "Sara, you can go back to bed. Everything is safe again. Your dad is downstairs if you need him." Sara went to her room as Rick led Kate back to bed.

"I know you have been through a lot today, Kate, but rest assured that Will and I are going to work on securing this home and farm from strangers. Today was an eye-opener, and I vow to protect you and little Sara."

"I shot him. I had no choice. I had to protect Sara. I have never killed someone before. I am a nurse. I heal people." Kate put her face in her hands and started sobbing.

Rick grabbed Kate's shoulder. "Listen to me, Kate. You did what you had to do. You saved yourself and Sara, and that was a brave thing to do. I wish I had been here to protect you. For that I am sorry." Rick reached for Kate and held her in his arms. "You need rest. You sleep knowing you did the right thing!" Rick lay down with Kate still in his arms until she finally fell asleep.

*****

The next morning Will and Rick told Kate about their plans to secure the farm.

"What would you like for me to do?" she asked.

"I think you should just rest," Rick answered.

"No, I want to be busy. Tell me how I can help," Kate insisted.

"Inventory what food supplies we have in the house and in the root cellar. We need to have a good supply of food if we need to shelter down inside. Also, if you could go up into the attic and see if there are any bells."

Kate looked puzzled. "Bells?"

"Yes, like maybe Christmas bells. We need them to hang on the front, back, and side doors. They will chime if someone is trying to get in the door."

Kate headed for the attic.

"What can I do, Uncle Rick?" Sara had heard them talking.

"Find as many empty jars as possible with lids. We will need them to store water." Sara nodded and went down to the basement.

Rick and Will went out to the barn to get some fencing and the rest of the barbed wire. Will started in the front yard, heightening the fence and adding some wire around the top. Rick was strengthening the fence around the back of the house and the garden, also adding some barbed wire.

Kate found an old cowbell and some Christmas bells in the attic; she also found a couple of paddle locks with keys in an old trunk. She placed the cowbell on the front door and the Christmas bells on the back and side doors. "These locks will be great." Kate motioned Rick from the back porch.

"What's up?" he asked.

Kate showed him the paddle locks and suggested to use them for the greenhouse and pump house. "That's a good idea. Please hang the keys where we can find them in the kitchen." Rick took the locks and headed back out.

Sara was down in the basement and had already found a few jars. Kate came in. "What chore did Uncle Rick give you?"

Sara answered by holding up one of the jars. "We need to be able to store some water."

Kate smiled. "Good plan."

She continued into the root cellar to take inventory. As she worked there in the quiet, except for the occasional rattle of a jar from Sara, she couldn't stop thinking about shooting Ken. She closed her eyes for a moment. "I need to think of pleasant things." She started remembering the other night with Will, the kissing, and the touching. She opened her eyes; the memories brought her a warm feeling, but they also threw her off balance. She and Rick had been married so long. He provided her with such a feeling of security and reliability. They had been through a lot in their lives, but Will brought such a feeling of warmth, fun, and great passion that she hadn't felt in a long while. She was so conflicted, torn between Rick and Will. Each man had his own appeal. She had never strayed from Rick in their marriage; she had always been faithful. So why now the attraction to Will? Was it that she had become too comfortable with Rick and Will brought her excitement? Was it just a crush?

"Aunt Kate!" Sara interrupted Kate's thoughts.

She turned. "Yes, Sara."

"What do you want me to do with these jars?"

Kate stood. "Let's take them upstairs, wash them, and fill them with water," she instructed.

Will had finished the fence around the front. He went around the back of the house to see if Rick needed any help. "I finished the front fence. You need some help back here?"

"Why don't you get some chicken wire and cover the first floor windows?" Rick instructed.

Will nodded and went down to the barn to get some chicken wire. The wire would make it more difficult for others to climb through the windows and keep rocks and other projectiles from entering the house. He would start with the kitchen windows. When he went into the kitchen, Kate and Sara were at the sink filling the jars with water.

"What are you going to do, Dad?" Sara asked, placing a full jar of water on the counter.

"Just going to secure up our windows down here. Don't let me interrupt your work," he said, smiling at the two ladies. Kate and Sara returned to filling jars.

He stood there for a minute looking at Kate and his mind wandered to the other night. He remembered her soft skin, the sweet smell of her hair, and the passion of their kiss. He shook his head to help clear his mind, remembering this was his brother's wife. He returned to his work.

Kate and Sara had finished filling up the jars of water. "Aunt Kate, do you think this is enough water?"

"Well, we have quart-sized jars, and there are twelve. There are four of us. That would be enough for us to have one quart of water a day for three days at a minimum. I think I remember seeing some more canning jars in the attic when I was up there. Let's go up and see if we can find them," Kate answered Sara.

As they started for the attic, Rick came in the back door.

"Where are you two ladies heading?" Rick asked as he sat at the kitchen table.

"To look for some more canning jars up in the attic," Kate replied.

"Before you go, how does the inventory of our food supply look?" he asked, waving Kate over.

"We have been stocking up for winter, so we have a good supply for now. It is something we are just constantly going to need to watch. Maybe set aside a few items to save for an emergency, if possible. It is hard to say."

"Good to know. I am going to go hook up some extra lights to the solar battery for the front and back porch and outside the barn. We need more light at night." Kate gave Rick the thumbs-up, and she and Sara continued up to the attic.

"Aunt Kate, why are we doing these 'security' things? That is what Uncle Rick calls them," Sara asked as she helped Aunt Kate bring down the ladder to the attic.

"Well, we need to make our farm safer as people from the city come here. They will be looking for food and shelter. We need to protect what we have here on the farm," Kate explained, climbing the ladder.

"Can't we just share?" Sara asked.

"That is a nice thought, Sara, but most likely people will try to take all of our things. Life is getting pretty tough, and people will want what we have. We need to protect it." Kate reached her hand out to help Sara up into the attic.

"They wouldn't try to hurt us, would they?" she asked.

"Yes, Sara, they might. I hate to say that, but it is the truth. So now where did I see those canning jars?" Kate tried to change the subject; she wanted Sara to know the truth but didn't want to dwell on it.

"Aha, there they are. Let's put these in that empty box and get them down to the kitchen. We can get them washed up and filled with water." Kate grabbed the box, and the pair started filling it with jars. After taking the jars downstairs and filling them with water, Kate started preparing dinner. Sara was upstairs putting laundry away. Will and Rick had come in and were cleaning up. It was starting to get dark.

The family gathered in the kitchen and sat down at the table for dinner. "Beans again," scoffed Sara.

"Yep!" Will replied. "And you're damn lucky to have them." He gave Sara the angry father look.

Rick interrupted, "We need to break up our night watch. Our eyes and ears need to be open at night. That is when intruders are most likely to strike. I think we should split the night into two shifts. That way we can stay awake."

Rick continued to explain his plan for rotating shifts at night, Rick and Will taking their assigned shift each night.

"Wait a minute," Kate said as she put down her spoon. "What about me? I am capable of taking a shift," she said, with a smug look on her face directed at Rick.

"OK, how about you do 9:00–12:00 a.m., I will cover 12:00–3:00 a.m., and Will 3:00–6:00 a.m.?" Rick conceded.

They all agreed.

"Now about weapons," Rick instructed, "I want the shotgun downstairs, rifle on the second floor of the house, and one in the barn. We need to make sure we have our handguns on us at all times while outside, Will."

Sara had become bored and put her head in her hand and sighed. "Sara, you can go listen to your music if you like." Kate gave her an excuse to leave the table.

"Well, if I am going to be taking the 3:00–6:00 a.m. shift, I should head to bed."

Will got up from the table and headed upstairs, following behind Sara. Kate got up and started to clear the table, and Rick stood and helped. The two did not say much to each other while they washed and dried the dishes.

Rick kissed Kate on the cheek. "I'm going to go lie down. I will be back down at midnight to take over the watch. Let me know if there are any problems."

Kate nodded and finished up in the kitchen and then went into the living room to sit on the couch. She sat there listening to the silence, reflecting how her life had changed so much. She missed people; working as a nurse, she had so much contact with others. Even though she had her family, she sometimes felt lonely. She turned the lights off and grabbed the shotgun and stepped out on the front porch in the dark. The night was so quiet and still. She sat down on a nearby chair, staring into the darkness of the night. The silence was interrupted by the sound of a bloodcurdling scream. It was coming from inside the house.

"Sara!" Kate ran in the house and up the stairs. Will was already in Sara's room, trying to wake her up.

"Sara! Wake up!"

"They are trying to get me, Dad! I keep running, and they keep following me!" Sara's eyes were wide open, and she was sweating.

"It's only a dream, Sara. You're safe," Will tried to reassure her. She sat up and looked over at Kate. "Aunt Kate, the men were trying to catch me."

Kate sat down beside Sara on the bed, taking her in her arms. "Hush now, it's OK. I understand you're scared, but you are safe. How about your dad stays here with you for a while?"

Kate looked over at Will. She stood and traded places with him and quietly walked out and closed the door. Kate knew all the talk about security, people trespassing and trying to get in the house, seemed to be too much for Sara. Maybe a smaller version of the truth might be better for her.

"Is she OK?" Rick walked beside Kate.

"For now, but I don't fault her for being afraid. I know I am." Kate went back down the stairs. She grabbed the shotgun from the porch and closed and locked the front door. She leaned up against the door and began to cry, purely out of frustration.

CHAPTER NINE

THE WINDMILL

THE SUMMER HAD REMAINED HOT and quiet. John never did come back to the house looking for Ken, and it was slowly becoming an event of the past. Kate and Sara had been busy canning fruits and vegetables for the winter, and Kate had been teaching Sara to sew. Sara had even started a patchwork quilt out of old pairs of jeans they had found in the attic. Will and Rick had been busy with the corn crop. Kate often thought of how it just seemed like they had gone back in time, but when she could not simply go outside in the sunshine, the ways of the world creeped up on her again. She was enjoying the "secret balcony" as Sara called it, where they were able to enjoy the sun in secret.

Will and Rick had been working on the windmill out in the pasture, which they depended on for water in the fields. A few of the sails on the windmill needed replacing; the wind and rain had done damage over the years.

"I'm going to ride out to see if I can savage some sails from any old windmills out in the valley," Will said. He had already saddled his horse and was ready to go.

"If that doesn't work, I can go see what I can find in Jefferson," Rick said.

As Will rode off, Rick let the other horse out into the pasture and then went up to the house to get out of the sun for a while.

When Rick came in the back door to the kitchen, Kate yelled, "Hey, stay out of the kitchen, mister!" Kate was baking a cake, as today was

Rick's birthday. She had saved the last of the sugar they had and was using it for the cake. It wouldn't have frosting, but it would be sweet and a special treat.

"OK, OK, I am just going to go upstairs," Rick consented.

Sara laughed. "He has no idea, does he, Aunt Kate?"

"Nope," she replied.

"Did you finish his birthday present?" Sara asked. Kate had taken apart some old shirts from the attic and fashioned a new shirt for Rick.

"It's all done," Kate said as she indicated some wrapping paper on the table. "Do you want to wrap it up?"

"Sure!" Sara said as she took the paper. "Where is the shirt?"

"In the top drawer of the cabinet next to the sewing machine," Kate said. Sara retrieved the shirt, wrapped it carefully, and laid it on the counter next to the birthday cake.

"How about we put these in the cupboard and hide them till after dinner?" Kate proposed.

"Great idea!" Sara responded as they put the cake and the shirt in the cupboard.

*****

Will had been riding most of the day when he finally came upon a windmill. Looking around, he saw no animals in the pasture and, more importantly, no people. He jumped down from his horse and got started going through the windmill and seeing what sails he could salvage for parts. He worked throughout the afternoon and started packing what he had found.

He saw movement out of the corner of his eye and noticed off in the distance a man on a horse riding toward him. He climbed up on his horse and got his rifle ready. When he finally got a clear view of the man, he noticed it was Eli and decided to ride up to meet him.

"Hello, Eli, how are you doing?" Will greeted him.

"Will, I am well, and you?" Eli tipped his hat.

"Not doing too bad," Will obliged, "just out here looking for some parts to repair our windmill. How are you and your family doing?"

"We are running low on supplies, so I am off to Jefferson to see if I can trade for what we need. We did well with the corn, so I have some to trade." Eli smiled and pointed at a couple of large sacks of corn strapped to his horse.

"I wish you luck, young man, and say hello to your dad for me. And, Eli, be careful," Will said, tipping his hat before the two men rode off in opposite directions.

When Will reached home that evening, he put the horse along with all the parts he had found for the windmill in the barn and headed up to the house, where Rick was outside sitting on the porch.

"Were you able to find any sails for the windmill?" he asked.

"Yes, I stripped down one I found way down the valley," Will answered, "which should fix the problem." He sat down next to Rick on the porch. "I ran into Eli. He was on his way to Jefferson. He had some corn to trade, said they were running low of supplies." Will paused. "By the way, happy birthday, old man!" Will said, slapping Rick on the back and laughing.

"Geez, thanks," Rick replied.

"So what does Kate have planned?" Will asked.

"Nothing, I guess," Rick said, standing up, "which is fine with me. I do not need reminding that I'm getting older."

Rick walked back into the house, Will followed him, and as they entered, they could both smell dinner cooking. They passed through into the dining room, where Sara was just finishing setting the table.

"Do you gentlemen have a reservation?" Sara asked with a big smile.

"We sure do!" Will said, picking up Sara and swinging her around. "We are the Campbell party!"

Kate walked in carrying a nice roasted chicken, which was a very rare special meal.

"Sara, can you go get the potatoes?" she instructed. Sara nodded and headed off to the kitchen.

"Anything I can help you with?" Will asked.

"If you could bring in the green beans, we'll be all set," Kate said, setting the chicken down in the center of the table. Rick pulled out the chair so Kate could sit.

"Your chair, madam," he offered.

"Why, thank you, kind sir," Kate replied and sat down as Rick pushed in her chair. Will and Sara returned from the kitchen with the rest of dinner.

"Please, everyone, sit down, and let's enjoy this great-looking meal our lovely ladies have prepared," Rick said, motioning to the dinner before them. Everyone sat down and joined hands, and Rick said the dinner blessing.

"Amen. Now let's eat!" Will said, digging into the potatoes.

"I helped pluck the feathers off the chicken," Sara said proudly.

"Nice job, pumpkin," Will said.

"Everything is delicious," Rick added.

"It is a special occasion, you know?" Kate said, smiling at Rick.

"You don't have to remind me it's my birthday. I am already feeling old today," Rick said with an unpleasant look on his face.

"You're not old, just twenty-one with a lot of experience." Kate laughed.

"I know it has been a rough year, but we are here together, safe, with food on the table, and healthy, so let's celebrate another year of life!"

Kate got up and went into the kitchen and brought back the cake and Rick's birthday gift.

"I knew Kate would have a plan," Will said, winking at Kate. Kate handed Rick his gift; he smiled and started to open it.

"Oh, it's a shirt," Rick said, holding it up.

"Aunt Kate worked really hard on that, Uncle Rick. That old sewing machine doesn't always work very well," Sara explained.

"It's nice. Thank you, Kate," Rick said, wrapping the shirt back up.

"Are you going to try it on?" Kate asked. "I might need to alter it."

"Maybe later," Rick responded. Kate looked disappointed.

"Let's have some of that cake," Will said, rubbing his stomach and smiling.

Kate and Sara cut and served the cake, then Kate started to clear the dishes.

"Aren't you going to have some cake, Kate?" Will asked.

"Maybe later," Kate said, smirking at Rick. Everyone but Kate sat there, quietly finishing their cake.

"Sara, are you finished?" Will asked.

"Yes, Dad," Sara responded.

"Please go help Aunt Kate with the dishes," Will said, looking over at Rick. Sara picked up the rest of the dishes and skipped off to the kitchen.

"What the hell is your problem?" Will asked Rick as he threw down his napkin and stood up.

"What are you insinuating?" Rick demanded.

"I don't understand why you treat Kate the way you do," Will declared. "She goes to the trouble of making a delicious dinner, cake, and a gift for your birthday, and you can barely crack a smile. You couldn't be bothered to even try the shirt on even though Kate clearly wanted you to. What the hell, Rick!"

Rick sighed, "Let me explain this to you. It's that I don't like Kate giving Sara all these wrong ideas of happy birthdays, cakes, and gifts. That's not the real world. She needs to know that things are hard, that life is going to be a real struggle."

Will looked at Rick. "Life isn't all drudgery. It's hard work, sure, but there's also good times." Rick walked over to Will.

"I know Kate has taught Sara well," Rick agreed. "It's just that I think she needs to toughen her up, be more realistic."

Will insisted, "But this isn't just about the birthday, Rick. Why are you so cold to Kate? All she wants is some attention. Even I can see that."

"Well, I think you just need to mind your own damn business," Rick said, shoving Will back down in his chair. Kate had heard the raised voices, and she could hear the two men arguing. Sara came up behind her.

"Is everything OK, Aunt Kate?" Sara asked. "Uncle Rick was kind of being an asshole tonight."

"Sara!" Kate admonished her. "Well, I guess you're right. He has been kind of an ass tonight." They looked at each other. Sara went up to her room to read, and Kate went up to the balcony. It was hot, and she wanted to sit outside. She was trying to keep from getting upset over the events of the evening. As she sat there, she decided to try to snuggle up to Rick in bed and see if he would respond. It had been a long while since they had been romantically together.

While Kate was out on the balcony, Rick had come back in; he was lying in bed when she came into the bedroom. She slipped out of her clothes and crawled in beside Rick, cuddling up close and wrapping her arms around him. She gently kissed him on the neck but got no response. She kissed him again and nibbled at his ear but again got no response. Rick rolled away from her.

"Kate, it is just too hot for that tonight," he reprimanded her.

Kate moved over to her own side of the bed, tears welling up in her eyes. Kate got up, put her clothes back on, and headed out the door. As she left the room, Will stuck his head out of Sara's room.

"Kate?" he offered. "Everything OK?" Kate just shook her head and ran down the stairs. Will could hear the kitchen door shut. He went over to the window in Sara's room and saw Kate running toward the woods.

"Sara, maybe you should head to bed," he suggested.

"What's going on?" she asked.

"Nothing to worry about." Will patted her on the top of the head and left down the stairs.

He had seen Kate heading north, toward the river. He went down to the barn and grabbed a horse and took off after Kate. There was enough light from the full moon to illuminate the path she had taken.

Kate reached the river. She undressed and jumped into the water; it felt cool and good on this hot night. A few minutes later, Kate heard a horse approaching, so she swam up behind a rock to hide.

She remained quiet and still and out of sight.

"Kate, are you here? Where are you?" Will asked her as he got down from his horse. Kate swam out from behind the rock.

"I'm over here," she offered. Will took off his shirt and pants and dived in the water.

"Wow, that feels good," he said. Kate swam up to him.

"I have sneaked down here to the river a few times but only at night. Please don't tell Rick. He would not approve," she pleaded.

"I wouldn't think of it, but—" Will started until Kate put her fingers to his lips.

"Let's not talk about what happened," Kate said. "Let's just enjoy the moonlit night, the stars, and the cool water." Kate splashed water at Will.

"Why, you little shit," Will said as he swam after Kate.

Initially she swam away. Then she stopped and turned around; he came up to her. She put her hands on his chest and kissed him hard. He returned the passion. He pulled back and looked at Kate in the moonlight. Will had only been with his wife in the last twelve years, so to be experiencing such want and desire from another woman was a bit awkward but most welcome. She kissed him and then slid her hands down his back, drawing him closer. He kissed her down her neck, and she moved her hands down to feel his ass. He responded by kissing her breast; she tipped her head back and enjoyed the feeling of his lips on her skin. She could feel his desire grow as he pressed up against her body. He lifted her from the water and brought her to the grassy shore and laid her down. He sat beside her.

"You know I love you?" he asked with a smile.

"I love you too," she said as she reached for him and pulled him down. He put his hands down between her thighs and up to her wetness and desire. He wanted her, and she moaned with the pleasure of two bodies joining. She could now feel him inside her and looked at his face; he looked so full of emotions. She closed her eyes to immerse herself in the feeling of being with him. Their desire peaked, and he slid down beside her and wrapped his arms and legs around her.

They lay there in each other's arms looking up at the moon. Will thought how wonderful it was to have a woman love and desire him. He did not want to let her go; he kissed her on the forehead. She looked up and smiled.

"I could lie here forever, but we should get back," Kate suggested. They grabbed their clothes and got dressed. Will walked over and untied the horse.

"Did you hear that?" he asked Kate.

"Yes, it sounds like footsteps." Will grabbed Kate's hand and pulled her to him.

"Who's there?" he asked. They heard the rustle of footsteps again. "Who's there?" Will asked louder. Then a small boy, no more than five or six years old with blond hair and very thin, walked out from behind the trees. His clothes were dirty and his hair matted.

"Do you have any food?" the boy asked shyly. Kate leaned down to talk to the boy.

"Sure, we do, but where is your daddy?" she asked.

Will was scouting the area, looking for anyone who might be with the boy but found no sign of anyone.

"I don't know," he answered, putting his head down. "My mommy died." Will picked the boy up.

"I am sorry to hear that," he said, trying to console the boy. "My mommy is gone too. How long have you been out here in the woods?" The boy looked down at his hands and held up five fingers.

"Five days, that is a while." Will put the boy on his horse. Kate and Will looked at each other, then looked around again to see if there were any signs of anyone with the boy, but they saw nothing.

"Should we take him home?" Will asked Kate.

"Of course," Kate replied, taking pity. "He looks hungry and in need of a bath. We can figure out where he has come from once we get him fed and cleaned up." She grabbed the reins of the horse and started walking back to the farmhouse. Will walked up beside her and took her other hand.

"Kate, I don't think we should bring the boy in the house," Will whispered to Kate. "We don't know where he came from, and we need to think about protecting Sara."

"I agree," Kate replied, "at least until we find out how he got here."

Reaching the barn, they opened the door and brought the horse with the boy inside.

"Here is a safe place for you," Kate said. "I am going to go get you something to eat. This is Will. He will stay with you. By the way, what is your name?"

"Pete," the boy replied.

"OK, Pete," Kate answered, "I'll be right back." Kate went to the house and into the kitchen. The house was dark.

"Where have you been?" Rick asked from where he was sitting at the kitchen table in the dark.

"Holy crap, Rick," Kate stammered and put her hand to her heart, "you scared the daylights out of me!" Kate paused a moment to recover herself.

Rick continued. "I saw you leave the house upset with me and Will following you. I stayed here to keep an eye on Sara."

Kate had to think of something. "Will found me down by the river. He had convinced me to come back to the house, then I heard someone crying. It sounded like a child. Will searched around and found a small boy in the woods. He was all alone."

"A boy?" Rick asked with a mix of skepticism and alarm. "How old?"

"He must be around five or six," she informed. "Will has him out in the barn." Kate started to make the boy something to eat.

"Where did he come from?" Rick continued.

"We're not sure," Kate answered. "He just said he didn't know where his dad was and that his mother had died. He was scared and hungry and asked for food. Rick grabbed the small plate of food she prepared.

"I'll take this out," Rick insisted. "I want you to stay in the house till we figure this out." Rick slammed the door on his way out. Kate waited a few minutes and followed. She went down to the barn and listened at the door.

"His name is Pete," she heard Will say.

"Hi, Pete, my name is Rick. It's nice to meet you. Here, I brought you something to eat." Pete grabbed the plate and started eating as fast as he could.

"Woah, slow down, Pete," Will instructed. "You don't want to choke."

Rick and Will questioned the boy for a while but did not get many more answers regarding where the boy had come from and who he belonged with. Rick was suspicious of the boy. After the boy finished his food, he fell fast asleep in the hay.

"Let's leave him here in the barn to sleep and go talk to Kate," Will proposed as he covered the boy with a horse blanket. Kate headed back to the house before the men would see her listening in on the conversation. Rick locked the barn on the way out.

"Why'd you do that?" Will asked.

"Do we really want him coming into the house and seeing Sara?" Rick questioned. "He already saw Kate."

"OK," Will agreed.

Sitting around the kitchen table, they all discussed the boy.

"What are we going to do?" Kate asked, concerned. "We can't just let him wander the woods."

"We can't let him stay here either," Rick countered. "We need to find out where he belongs."

"What if he has no one?" she asked.

"We'll just need to cross that bridge when we get to it," Rick replied decidedly. "Tomorrow I'll take the boy around to the neighboring farms. Will can stay here to see if anyone comes by looking for him."

"Well, he needs a bath and his clothes to be washed," Kate said.

"Let's have Will get a bath ready for him in the morning," Rick agreed, "and bring his clothes back to the house to be washed."

"Me?" Will said. Rick just looked at Will. "OK, I'll take care of it," Will conceded.

Back in the kitchen, Rick turned to Kate.

"That boy is going to tell whoever his family is that you are here," Rick let out. Kate just looked at him.

"There's nothing we can do about that now," Kate said.

*****

In the morning Will went and grabbed some soap and a towel and headed to the barn. He filled the water trough, woke the boy, and gave him the bar of soap.

Will soon returned with the boy's clothes.

"Pete keeps asking for you," Will told Kate as she started washing the boy's clothes. "I think he misses his mother."

"Poor thing," she said. "Here bring him an apple. And then come back to hang up these clothes to dry." Kate handed Will an apple.

"You would have been such a great mother," Will offered. "You have such a big heart." Kate blushed.

Will went back to the barn, helped the boy out of the bath, handed him a towel to dry himself, and then wrapped him up in the towel until his clothes were ready. He then gave the boy the apple from Kate.

"Can I go outside?" the boy asked. "I miss my mommy," he sobbed. "Can I see the lady?"

"You need to dry off and wait for your clothes, then my brother, Rick, is going to take you to see if he can find your family," Will answered.

"I want to see the lady," the boy started to cry again.

"Wait here." Will then went back up to the house to find Kate. She was in the kitchen.

"The boy is crying and really missing his mother," Will informed. "He asked if he could see you."

"Where is Rick?" she asked, looking around. "How about I bring him some cake left from Rick's birthday?" Kate sliced a piece of cake and then handed Will the boy's wet clothes to hang and then went down to the barn.

"Hello, Pete," Kate started. "I brought you a piece of cake. Are you hungry?"

“Yes, ma’am,” he replied, taking the cake. Kate brushed the hair out of the boy’s face.

“You look so handsome all cleaned up.” The boy smiled.

“Do I get to live with you?” the boy asked.

“First, we need to see if we can find your family,” she consoled. “I’m sure someone is missing you.”

Pete finished up his cake. Kate came over and sat beside him. In return, he leaned over and put his head on her shoulder. Kate heard someone coming into the barn; it was Will.

“The child is exhausted,” Kate said, looking up at Will. “He’s obviously been through a lot.”

Suddenly, Rick opened the barn door.

“There you are,” he hissed. Kate looked up at Rick as he grabbed her hand. “Let’s go!” he commanded as he led Kate back to the house.

Will remained with the boy.

They returned to the house, where Sara was in the kitchen fixing herself something to eat.

“What’s going on?” Sara asked when she saw them coming in through the door.

“Oh, I was just having your aunt Kate look at one of the horses,” Rick offered. “He has a wound on his leg.”

“Oh, OK,” Sara replied before sitting down. “Any cake left?”

Kate brought Sara the last piece of cake. As Sara ate, Kate began to worry that the boy had seen Will and her together at the river and that somehow Rick would find out. She got a knot in her stomach; she wasn’t sure whether it was because she was afraid of getting caught or it was from guilt.

*****

Rick returned to the barn and saddled up one of the horses. Will had brought Pete his dry clothes and had him all ready to go.

"You ready, young man?" Rick asked the boy before lifting him onto the saddle.

"I don't know where my family is," Pete answered, starting to cry. "I want to stay here."

"Wherever your family is, they're most likely missing you and most likely scared that you're hurt." Rick joined Pete in the saddle before turning to Will. "Take good care of the place while I'm gone."

"Will do," Will replied before watching Rick ride off with Pete, then headed back to the house to see Kate.

"Part of me hopes he doesn't find his family," Kate confessed. "I know it's selfish, but it would be nice to have another child around for Sara."

As Rick and Pete turned out onto the road, Rick began to worry the boy would tell someone that there was a woman living at their farm.

"So tell me about your dad," Rick started. "Do you look like him, or do you look like someone else in your family?" The boy was quiet. "Pete?" Rick prompted.

"I don't know my dad," Pete finally responded.

"OK," Rick pursued, "what about your grandparents? Were you living with them?"

"My granddaddy, he is big and mean," Pete let out. "But he taught me how to fish, which I don't really like."

"Did he teach you anything else?" Rick inquired.

"My uncle says he teaches me nothing but lies," Pete retorted.

"Lies about what?" Rick pursued.

"Oh, nothing," Pete responded before clamming up. "I don't want to talk anymore," he stated.

Rick decided against pushing him any further. Anyway, they were coming up on the first farmhouse, the one where John and Ken had said they were staying. The house looked empty as Rick got down from his horse.

"You just stay right up there for now," Rick instructed as he tied the horse to the porch, stepped up to the front door, and knocked.

"Is anyone home?" he called out as he looked through the windows. He could see the house was a mess with furniture tossed and garbage thrown everywhere. Rick tried the door and found it was open. He stepped inside.

"Is anyone here?" he called out again. All was quiet except for the wind whistling through the broken windows. Rick climbed back up on his horse.

"Well, Pete, it looks like we're on to Washington's old farm," he said before they continued on in silence until Rick investigated. "So, Pete, do you live on a farm? One like mine?" he asked in hopes of getting more clues to where he might live.

"It has a house and animals. Does that make it a farm?" the boy replied.

"Depends on what kind of animal. What kind are there? Like maybe cows?" Rick suggested.

"No, but we do have a dog. I like dogs." Pete grinned.

As they turned off the road, Rick could see someone walking up the drive to meet him. It was Eli.

"Stop!" the man yelled out. Rick stopped his horse.

"Hello, Eli!" Rick hollered back as Eli came closer. "It's Rick, from the Campbell farm." Eli tipped up his cowboy hat.

"Why, it sure is," he said as he stuck out his hand to shake Rick's. "What brings you down this way?"

"We found this young fellow in the woods at the back of our property," Rick explained, turning his horse so Eli could see the boy. "I'm just trying to find out where he belongs."

"Can't say I know the young fellow," Eli said before directing his attention to Pete. "What's your name?" he asked. Pete didn't answer.

"He doesn't have much to say these days," Rick offered. "He says his name is Pete."

"You know, he might belong down at that small farm a few miles from here," Eli said, pointing down the valley. "I saw some blond-haired people there the other day, and he sure is a towhead."

"Thanks, Eli," Rick replied as he turned his horse back toward the road. "Say hello to your dad for me, and you have a good day."

Rick and Pete rode on and then down to the river to stop for lunch.

Rick got down off the horse and lifted Pete down.

"We need to water the horse, and I'm hungry," Rick said. "What about you?"

Pete nodded.

"Let's see what we've got," Rick said as he reached into the saddlebag and pulled out a couple of biscuits.

"Let's sit down there along the bank, where we can wash our hands and eat in the shade while our horse has something to drink," Rick indicated as he led Pete down to a shaded area of grass next to the river. Rick handed the boy a biscuit.

"Thank you," Pete said, taking the biscuit without looking up at Rick. "I wish I could have a grandpa like you."

After they finished eating, Pete stood up and picked up a rock.

"Do you know how to make a rock skip across the water?" Rick offered as he found himself his own rock to use for demonstration. "You've already taken the first step, which is to find a nice flat rock. Now face the water at a slight angle," he continued as he demonstrated, "and with your arm low to the ground, throw your arm out and release the rock." Rick threw the rock, counting the number of times it skipped off the water. "See that!" Rick exclaimed. "Three times!" Pete smiled and clapped his hands.

"Now it's my turn!" he shouted as he threw his rock low across the water. "Three times too! Let's do it again!" Rick and Pete skipped stones and laughed, losing track of time for a while.

"Now that was fun!" Rick exclaimed. "But we need to go ahead and get to that last farmhouse." Rick helped Pete back up on the horse, then climbed up himself.

While they were riding, he was thinking about how much joy he had felt in teaching the boy something as simple as skipping stones. He began to understand why Kate enjoyed teaching Sara so much. Maybe he should not be so hard on her and be more understanding. They reached the farmhouse, and Eli was right, there was a family of blonds living on the farm.

"Hello," Rick greeted once they got within hearing distance. "Don't worry, I'm not here to cause any trouble. I'm just looking for the family of this young man." A thin older man holding a shotgun came up to Rick and the boy.

"We aren't missing a boy," the man stated curiously. "Where did you find him?"

"In the woods at the back of our farm," Rick replied. A younger man now approached.

"What is your name, young man?" he asked.

"Pete," said Pete.

"Pete what?" the man asked.

"Just Pete," Pete said, now holding on to Rick.

"We would be glad to keep him," the older man offered. "We could use another pair of hands around here." Rick backed up the horse a little.

"No, that's OK," he countered. "But thanks anyway for your offer." As they rode away, Pete turned and looked back at the two men. They had several young boys standing behind them. He grabbed on to Rick a little harder.

"Time to go home, Pete," Rick said as they turned out onto the road.

By the time Rick and Pete returned home, Pete had fallen asleep, leaning up against Rick.

"Glad you're back," Will said as he grabbed Pete, and Rick slid down from the saddle. "Kate was getting worried."

"Yes, well, as you can see, we didn't find the boy's home," Rick said. "If you don't mind, could you take the boy and the horse to the barn while I go inside to talk with Kate?"

"Sure," Will said as he turned toward the barn, and Rick walked up to the house.

"Rick, is that you?" Kate asked as he came in through the front door. Rick walked into the kitchen and up to Kate, and gave her a big hug.

"I am glad to be home," he said.

"Did you find the boy's family?" she asked.

"No, but he got to tell me a little bit about his family," Rick replied.

"How he didn't know his father and about how his grandfather and uncle were mean, and I started thinking he may be better off without them. Obviously they are not out looking for the boy." Rick leaned back from hugging her to look her in the eye, still holding his hands around her waist. "Would you object if he stayed here for a while? Until we hear news of his family?" Kate smiled.

"I would love for him to stay!" Kate beamed and kissed Rick on the cheek. "Where is he now?"

"He had fallen asleep, so Will took him out to the barn," Rick explained. "Let's let him sleep till morning. For now, I just want a bath and a soft bed." Rick kissed Kate and headed out to take a bath just as Will was returning to the house.

"So what did he say?" he asked her.

"He asked if the boy could stay," she beamed. "I said yes, of course!"

"Maybe we're beginning to see a new side of Rick," Will suggested. "Pete is a cute little fellow." Kate grabbed Will's hand.

"Can we introduce him to Sara in the morning?" she said excitedly.

"Don't see why not," he answered with a quick kiss on her lips.

When Kate went up to bed, Rick was already asleep. She went to the window and opened it before sitting down in the old rocking chair to feel the cool night air billow in. All she could think about was tomorrow and what she would do to settle Pete into the house.

*****

Morning came, and Rick woke up Kate, who had fallen asleep in the rocker.

"Oh, my neck!" Kate said, rubbing her neck.

"Well, you should have came to bed, silly," Rick said, laughing.

"Isn't that like the old saying, 'Do as I say, not as I do?'" she said, laughing back. They both got dressed and headed downstairs.

"I will go get the boy," Rick offered as he put his hat on and headed down to the barn. Kate started to cook some eggs, and Sara came down.

"Good morning, Aunt Kate," she said.

"Good morning, little miss," Kate replied. "We have a surprise for you today and one that's going to make things a little different around here."

"What is it?" Sara asked, now very curious. At that moment Will came into the room.

"Hey, sunshine!" Will greeted her as he picked her up and swung her around.

"I hear there is a surprise!" Sara said.

"Yes, there is," Will replied, looking over at Kate.

"I wasn't going to tell her without you," Kate said, handing Will a plate of eggs. At that moment Rick came running in.

"The boy is gone!" Rick shouted.

"What?" Kate ran to Rick.

"I went out to the barn, and he was gone!" he exclaimed.

"Kate, can you and Sara keep inside with the doors locked?"

The two men went down to the barn.

"I don't understand," Will said, picking up the blanket Pete had used and looking around. "Where could he have gone?" Rick noticed a couple of boards missing from the back of the barn.

"Look." Rick pointed it out to Will.

"There is no way Pete did that. He had to have help," Will added.

"I knew this whole thing seemed fishy from the beginning. We need to find that boy and whoever put him up to this!" They went around the back of the barn, where they could see a couple of sets of footprints, which led to horse hoofprints.

The two saddled up the horses, grabbed their shotguns, and tried to follow the hoofprints.

Back at the house, Kate explained to Sara about the boy.

"He was all alone?" she asked.

"Yes," Kate answered, "we are not sure where he came from. Uncle Rick went looking for his family yesterday but could not find them. We had decided to let Pete stay, and now he is gone."

"I am sure they will find him, Aunt Kate," Sara said, wrapping her arms around Kate.

The two men followed the hoof marks until they lost them. "I'm having trouble trying to follow these prints. I am not even sure they are the same prints we started with," Will concluded. "Let's ride over to the river, where I first found Pete."

He was hoping that maybe they had gone in that direction, but there was no sign of him or anyone. Eventually they returned to the farmhouse. Will took the horses into the barn as Rick went up to the house. Kate was waiting in the basement.

"Well?" she asked. Rick broke the news to her, leaving out the part about the broken barn boards and the footprints. He didn't want her to worry even more than she already was.

"I hope he will be all right," Kate said, holding back tears. "I do not understand why he wouldn't want to stay. It makes no sense." Rick sat down next to Kate and put his arms around her.

"I know," he consoled her as she snuggled into his chest. "The boy was starting to grow on me too." Rick sat quietly, just holding her. "I should go talk to Will."

"OK," Kate agreed.

When Rick arrived, he found Will sitting in the barn.

"I just don't get it," Will said, shaking his head.

"I'm sure someone took him," Rick suggested. "That last family I talked with, the blond-haired ones, seemed pretty shady. I think I'll pay them a visit," Rick said, grabbing his saddle and throwing it up on his horse, then taking a moment to check his gun. "You should be prepared too. There might be trouble." Will nodded as Rick mounted his horse and took off.

As he approached the Washington farm, he went up to the house to see if they had seen the boy. When he arrived at the house, Eli and Chris were doing some work to the house. Rick jumped down from his horse.

"Hello, Mr. Campbell," Eli greeted him as he stepped down from his ladder.

"Mr. Campbell was my dad's name," Rick replied. "You can call me Rick."

The two laughed. "How's it going, Rick?" Chris stuck out his hand, then gave Rick a pat on the back. At that time Chris's father, Wes, came out to the porch. "Rick, this is my father, Wes."

Rick shook his hand. "Nice to meet you."

"Thanks for the horse. It has been a godsend," Wes acknowledged. "It was a good trade." Rick smiled. The men sat down on the porch.

"Eli told me you were by yesterday with a young boy looking for his family," Chris interjected.

"Yes," Rick confirmed, "but then yesterday evening he went missing. I'm going to check the farm down the road for him."

"That is a strange bunch," Chris said. "You shouldn't go alone. Eli and I will be glad to go along. It's the least I could do for you not kicking my son's ass when he showed up at your farm." The men laughed.

"Well, thanks for the offer, but I don't want to cause you any trouble."

"Oh, we like a little trouble now and then." Chris chuckled.

They put a bridle on their horse, and the two climbed up. "Watch your back!" Wes yelled as the three men rode off down the road.

When they arrived at the farmhouse, it looked like no one was around.

"If you two want to try the barn," Rick proposed, "I'll try the house."

"Sure," Chris replied. Rick got down from his horse and stepped onto the porch. He knocked on the door, and a small boy answered.

"Who is it?" yelled a man from another room.

"It's the man that was here yesterday, sir!" the boy hollered back.

"What's he want?" the man said, coming to the door.

"I'm sorry to bother you," Rick placated. "Remember the boy I had with me yesterday?"

"Of course," the man retorted, spitting on the floor, "or do you think I'm ignorant?" By then the room had several boys and the young man from yesterday in it, standing there, staring at Rick. "Have you seen him?"

"Lost him already, did ya?" The man laughed.

"Hey, any of you seen the young fella from yesterday?" he asked as he looked around the room. Chris came up and joined Rick on the porch.

"Looks like you have a friend with you," said the man, lifting his shotgun.

"I'm not here for any trouble," Chris confided as he held up his hands. "I'm just helping my friend look for the boy."

Eli, meanwhile, had gone around to the back of the house. He looked in the back window into the kitchen, which he saw was empty. He stepped up on the back porch stairs; they creaked, and he stopped. He could still hear them talking on the front porch, so he continued up the stairs. He tried the back door; it was locked. He looked in the porch window and still saw no one in the kitchen.

"We haven't seen the boy since yesterday," said the young man.

"Best you be leaving," the other man added, gripping his gun, "before I shoot!"

"OK, we're happy to oblige," Rick said as he and Chris backed off the porch. "Thank you for your assistance." They climbed up on their horses and rode back up the driveway, where they found Eli waiting for them.

"I went up to the back porch and had a look around," Eli recounted. "All I saw was there were six plates on the kitchen table."

"Well, there was six of them all together," Chris remembered.

"I don't think the boy is there," Eli said, shaking his head. "Sorry."

The men started back home. When they reached the Washington farm, Rick thanked them for helping him out. "If you happen to see the boy, let me know." Rick tipped his hat and rode off.

Rick's main concern right now was that Pete would mention Kate to whoever took the boy, which at this time he was pretty sure it was his grandfather and that this whole situation looked like some kind of setup. He was going to have to really lock down Kate and Sara to the house for their own safety. He returned home.

"Did you find the boy?" Kate asked hopefully.

"No, I'm sorry, Kate, but the boy is gone."

CHAPTER TEN

PITCHFORK

FALL WAS IN THE AIR, and the leaves were beginning to change color. Kate and Sara were busy preserving and storing fruits and vegetables in the root cellar for the winter months, while Will was adding some shelves to store more supplies. Rick was outside cutting wood to stock up for the winter. Sara went down to the basement with a handful of jars to put on the shelf.

"Hey, Dad, here are some jars for the shelf."

"Perfect timing!" Will said as he pounded the last nail.

"Dad, can I ask you a question?" Sara said as she sat down.

"Of course, and always," Will said with a smile.

"Are you in love with Aunt Kate?" Will dropped one of the jars. "What?" he said as he bent down to clean up the mess.

"Are you in love with Aunt Kate?" Sara asked again.

"Wow, that is a loaded question," Will said, squatting down next to Sara.

"It's OK if you are," Sara added. "I love her too."

"Yes, I love Kate," he answered. "She is part of our family."

"You know that's not my question," Sara insisted. Just then Kate walked in carrying more jars for the shelf.

"Hey, you two, are you sitting down on the job?" She laughed. Will was glad for the interruption.

"We were just taking a quick break," he consented. "I'm all finished with the shelves."

"Nice," Kate said, setting her jars up on the shelf. "How about tonight we watch that movie Rick found in Jefferson?"

"Great idea!" Will said.

"What movie was it?" Sara asked.

"*Mrs. Doubtfire*," Kate replied.

"That's one of my favorites," Sara said, excited.

"We'll set it up after dinner. We should have enough power in the solar battery. Could you come up with me and set the table?"

Sara followed Kate up the stairs but, before reaching the top, looked back at Will and said, "I still would like an answer, Dad."

Will smiled. "I know."

After dinner they all sat down to watch the movie. Kate had popped some popcorn that she had been saving on the stove. Rick sat in his usual place in the recliner, leaving the couch for the others. After Kate had sat down on one end, Sara quickly sat down on the opposite end so that Will would have to sit next to Kate. They were all enjoying the movie when they heard someone—or something—come up to the house. Rick shut off the movie and signaled for Kate and Sara to go down to the basement.

"Rick, this is Eli Washington!" Eli yelled. "My father has been hurt badly!"

Rick opened the door. He could see Eli at the fence trying to hold up Chris, who had blood all over the side of his right leg.

"What happened?" Rick shouted as he grabbed ahold of Chris and helped Eli bring him inside the house.

"I had gone up to the house, and Dad was putting the horse in the barn," Eli relayed, "and there was a man inside the barn trying to take our cow. He stabbed Dad in the leg with the pitchfork and then took off."

"Let's get him downstairs," Rick said, nodding at Will. "Will, you open the door and go down first."

Will went down first and got Kate and Sara hidden in the armoire.

"Put him on the cot over there." Will pointed. They placed Chris on the cot, and Rick cut off his jeans from above the wound.

"Hand me that gauze, Will," Rick said, then placed the gauze over the three puncture wounds to try to stop the bleeding.

"Eli, why don't you come upstairs with me," Will suggested, "while we let Rick see what he can do to help your father?"

"Yes, Eli, please go with him," Chris agreed, "so Rick can work."

Will put his hand on Eli's shoulder. "Let's go get you a drink of water."

As soon as they were gone, Rick went to get Kate. She was already out of the armoire but told Sara to stay. "I know he is going to see me, but we don't have a choice," Kate said, pushing by Rick.

"He is bleeding pretty badly," Rick agreed. He lifted the gauze to show Kate.

"Hey, you're a woman!" Chris shouted.

"Chris, this is my wife, Kate," he introduced.

Kate placed new gauze over the wounds.

"Rick, hold as much pressure as you can," she instructed. "We need to stop the bleeding. I'm going to the medical cabinet to get some saline to clean the wounds and some clean towels to place under his leg."

Kate returned and lifted the gauze to get another look at the wounds.

"Looks like you got stabbed with something," Kate said. "Rick, lift his leg carefully so I can put the towels under it."

Kate placed the towels, then proceeded to clean the wounds.

"I was stabbed with a pitchfork," Chris explained.

"Great, a dirty pitchfork," Kate replied. "We need to get this as clean as possible."

Kate grabbed another bottle of water.

"Do you have something for pain?" Chris pleaded. "It's killing me!"

Kate finished cleaning the wounds and covered them with gauze.

"I'm going to start an IV and give you some pain medication and antibiotics," Kate said as she went over to the cabinet and grabbed what she needed.

"Are you a doctor?" Chris asked.

"She's an RN, and a damn good one too," Rick answered.

"A nurse and a woman, you're a lucky man," Chris said as he closed his eyes, and Kate started the IV.

"Your pain should fade here soon," she said. "Just get some sleep."

Chris mumbled something and then drifted off to sleep.

"Can I come out now that he is asleep?" Sara asked, cracking open the armoire door and peeking out. "It's getting cramped in here."

"Oh sorry! Yes, you can come out," Rick said before turning to Kate. "I'm going to go upstairs to let Eli know his father is resting."

Upstairs, Eli was pacing.

"Can I see him?" Eli asked, starting toward the basement door.

"In a moment. First, we need to explain a couple of things," Will interjected, stopping Eli before he reached the door. Will looked at Rick.

"Actually, I think the best way to explain is just to take him downstairs and let him meet Kate," Rick said, then opened the basement door.

"Kate?" asked Eli.

Will stopped Rick.

"What about Sara?"

"I think it will be safe to let them in on our secret," Rick said, "and unavoidable."

Will looked at Rick in shock, not because he hadn't come to trust Chris and Eli but because he had never expected Rick to be the one to realize it. The three men went down the stairs, where Kate and Sara were tending to Chris.

"Eli, this is Kate," Rick introduced, "and the girl helping her is Will's daughter, Sara. They have been taking care of your father."

"Hello, Eli," Kate said, extending her hand to shake his before Sara did the same. "Your father is going to be fine. We've cleaned his wounds and are giving him some pain medication and antibiotics." Eli walked up to his father. "Right now he is sleeping."

Eli sat down in the chair next to the cot.

"I guess that explains why you never invited me into the house!" Eli said, smiling.

"I think we all need some sleep," Kate offered, handing Eli a pillow and a blanket. "If you like, you can stay down here to keep an eye on him."

"Yes," Rick added, "we can discuss all this further in the morning."

Eli accepted the blanket and pillow.

"Thank you all so much for helping my dad."

Kate smiled. "No problem."

Once upstairs Kate confided in Rick, "You surprised me. I never would have thought you would let any man know about me."

Rick took Kate's hand and spoke from the heart. "I am sorry. I should have asked you first."

"No, you did the right thing bringing him to me," Kate rejoined. "And not all people in the world have bad intentions."

Rick wrapped his arms around Kate and consented, "We need friends and allies in today's world."

She kissed him gently on the lips.

"Chris is right," Rick said, kissing her back, "I am lucky to have you."

Everyone, tired from all the commotion, went off to bed.

*****

In the morning Kate went down to the basement to check on Chris.

"There she is!" Chris said, sitting up.

"Once again, thank you so much for helping my father," Eli said as he stood to shake Kate's hand.

"It was my pleasure," Kate replied. "Now let me take a look." Kate unwrapped Chris's wounds. "How is the pain?" she asked.

"It hurts but not as bad as last night," Chris said.

Kate went to the cabinet and got some new bandages and wrapped up the wounds.

"I'm going to give you some bandages to take home with you." She continued. "I want you to change them twice a day and come see me right away if you notice any bright redness or pus, that it starts to bleed again, or you have a fever or any other signs of infection, OK?"

Chris took the bandages and responded in gratitude, "Yes, I will." He added, indicating Sara and her, "And I want you to know that your secret is safe with us. We will not tell anybody about you and Sara." Chris went on to tell the story about his wife and how she had also survived the virus. One day some men had kidnapped her from the house while he and Eli were out in the barn. "Eli and I returned to the house, and the back door was open. We ran in and found tables and chairs tossed, and my wife was nowhere to be found." The two men looked continuously for her for days but could not find any sign of where they might have taken her. "I blamed myself. I didn't protect her or keep her safe," Chris said.

At that point Rick walked in. "I understand how you feel, Chris. Kate often tells me I am overprotective of her, but see, Kate, bad things happen."

Kate put her hand on Chris's shoulder. "I take it she is still missing?"

With tears in his eyes, Chris continued his story. "One day she returned to the house. She had gotten away from the men. She was beaten, bruised, her clothes torn, and her lips split."

At that point Eli walked away. Chris said that his wife did not speak a word. She went to take a bath, locked the door, and would not let Chris in the room. He was angry at what the men had done to his wife; he wanted revenge. He prepared his shotgun and was ready if they returned to steal back his wife. Finally, after a few days, his wife spoke.

"I am sorry. I should not have let those men take me and do horrible things to me. I was weak."

Chris took her hands. "You are not weak. You are strong and a survivor. This was not your fault. I should have protected you. I am the one who is sorry. No one will ever take you again."

Eli walked back over to join the conversation. "My mother was deeply scarred by what happened to her, and I am not just talking physically but emotionally. The days following, she just was not herself anymore, rarely smiled." He continued saying that she was always afraid; she would not want to be out of his father's sight for a moment. "One morning my father and I were in the kitchen starting breakfast. We both thought it was unusual for Mother to be in bed this long. I went upstairs to check on her. When I entered the bedroom, I found her. She had hanged herself." Eli started to cry, and Kate came and hugged him.

"I am so sorry, Eli." Kate tried to comfort him. "Chris, I am so sorry you had to go through that horrific experience."

Chris hung down his head. "So you see we totally understand. We will not let anyone know you are here. We will protect you at all costs."

Rick put his hand on Chris's shoulder. "I appreciate that very much, Chris. I am so sorry for your loss. Did the men ever return?" he asked.

"No, we've never seen anyone, and that was many months ago."

Eli helped his dad to stand. "We should get home so Dad can rest."

Rick helped Eli get Chris up the stairs. Kate followed them up the stairs. "Chris, I will send Rick by in a couple days to check on you, but if it gets very painful, swollen, red, or hot to the touch, Eli, you bring him right back," Kate instructed.

"I sure will, and thanks again." Eli gave Kate a smile, and he and his father started for home.

"Kate, you never seem to stop amazing me, a woman of such talent," Will said, smiling.

"Thanks, Will, but you're going to make me blush," she said, laughing.

"I've got things to do. See you two later," Will said while heading out the door.

Kate turned to Rick. "That was a terrible story about Chris's wife."

"Yes, it was," he replied.

"Can you make me a promise?" she asked.

"Depends on what the promise is," Rick said with a smile.

"If I was in the same situation as Chris's wife, being taken or kidnapped, and you were able, I would want you to shoot me," Kate said, looking directly into Rick's eyes.

"What? Are you crazy?" Rick shouted.

Sara had heard the commotion and came up to the kitchen door to listen.

“No, I am not crazy. I am serious.” Kate went on to say that if she were in that situation, she would not want to suffer from what would happen to her, what terrible things would be done to her; she would rather die than be put through such horror. She walked up to Rick and put her hands on his chest and looked him in the eyes. “If you loved me, you would not want me to suffer such things, such abuse and pain.”

Rick looked down at Kate. “I do love you and would not want to lose you either way. I do not want to think of such things,” he said, pulling her hands from his chest.

“But, Rick, you need to understand,” Kate pleaded.

“Stop! I do not want to discuss this. It’s morbid.” Rick walked away.

CHAPTER ELEVEN

KATE'S TRIP TO JEFFERSON

IN THE MORNING RICK MET Will in the barn.

"We need to butcher one of the steers and get the meat stored for the winter," Rick said, looking over at one of the steers.

Rick and Will knew if they were going to butcher a steer, they would have to have a way to preserve the meat for a long period. They did have the solar panels and battery to run the refrigerator, but they needed another way to be sure they would have a long-term meat supply. After the brothers did some disagreeing about how to accomplish this, they decided they would turn one of their small wooden storage sheds on the property into a smokehouse, a small one-room square structure where the rafters were exposed along the roof to hang the meat. In the middle of the room, they would construct a firepit, where they could build a fire to smoke the meat.

"Have you ever butchered a steer?" Will asked.

"Pretty much the same as field dressing a deer, and we used to hunt with Dad when we were teenagers. It's been a while, but I am sure we can handle it," Rick said, raising his eyebrows. "Let's get started."

Kate was in the basement inventorying her medical supplies. She had used many of them caring for Will's bullet wound, Mr. Washington's pitchfork punctures, and her own arm infection. She sat down on the cot to think. She knew that they needed more supplies, but where, and how?

"Kate! Kate!" Rick had come down to the basement. "Hello, Kate!" Rick said, waving at her.

Kate was staring off, thinking. "Oh, Rick, I am sorry. I was just thinking."

"Seems you were in deep thought. What's going on?" Rick sat next to Kate on the cot.

She stood and opened the cabinet doors. "Look, we are depleting our medical supplies. We need to restock. Just wondering how in the hell we are going to do that."

Kate knew the only place that they possibly could find some supplies would be the hospital in Jefferson. She knew the hospital had been shut down, but she still had her work keys. She sat back down next to Rick.

"I have got to go to Jefferson to the hospital and see what I can find. I still have my keys."

"There is no way I am letting you go to Jefferson. It is way too dangerous." Rick turned to Kate. "I will go!" he insisted.

"It would be best if I went along. I know where everything is. I know what keys belong to which storage rooms and cabinets." Kate stood, shutting the cabinet doors. "This is too important."

Rick went to Kate and put his arms around her. "Kate, I cannot let you do this. It is too risky."

The two continued to argue back and forth, each making their point, Kate regarding her going and Rick for her not. After a heated discussion, Kate finally informed Rick she was going with or without him. He had no choice but to concede. Now that they had the who and the where, it now was the how and when. There was a curfew in Jefferson, so no one was allowed out after dark. But during the day, there was a huge risk that someone would spot Kate as being a woman. Disguising her as a man worked from a distance, but if they were confronted up close, there was a high risk she would be discovered.

"I think at this point the only choice is to go at night, less chance of being confronted and discovered. We can use the darkness to our advantage," Rick pointed out to Kate; she agreed.

They would go tonight just after the sun set. They would double ride on the horse, leaving one at the farm in case they were captured. Will would still have a horse. They would dress in dark clothing, and both would carry a handgun for protection. Kate went upstairs to change; Rick went out to saddle up the horse. Will was out in the barn when Rick arrived.

"Will, I need to let you know our plans." Rick pulled the horse out from the stall.

"What plans? What are you talking about?" Will became curious. Rick told Will his plan. "That sounds dangerous, Rick. But I do understand the need for medical supplies. But are you sure? That puts Kate and you in a lot of danger," Will asked out of concern.

"Kate did not give me a choice. All I can do is protect her the best that I can." Rick continued to saddle his horse.

Will grabbed a canteen and filled it with water and handed it to Rick. "Good luck, brother."

Kate grabbed her backpack out of the closet; she needed something to carry the new supplies. She headed down the stairs and out to the barn; the sun had almost set. Will turned and looked at Kate as she entered the barn. He said nothing; he just walked up to her and hugged her tightly. She smiled.

"Please don't say anything to Sara. She is already asleep. I don't want her to worry. We should be back before the sun rises."

Rick mounted the horse and helped Kate up. Will opened the barn door, and the two rode off into the darkness.

"Thank you, Rick, for letting me come." Kate leaned against Rick with her arms around him.

"It's against my better judgment," he replied.

The two traveled along the river with the light of the full moon to guide them. It was a long ride, but they should reach Jefferson in plenty of time to get in the hospital, take what they need, and return home before the sun rises; at least that was the plan. When they got closer to town, they both slipped off the horse and tied it to a tree at the edge of town out of sight. They knew coming in on horseback would be too noticeable. Kate pulled the hood of her sweatshirt over her head and put her backpack on. Rick took her hand. "Stay close to me." Kate's heart was pounding; she had no idea what they were going to run into, hopefully no one.

The streetlights had no power, so it was dark. There were a few lanterns burning in windows, and at the end of the street was a barrel that had a fire burning in it. There were several men with guns standing around the barrel talking. The hospital was located in the center of the town.

"We need to find the best way to get around those men," Rick whispered to Kate.

"This way." Kate led Rick to an abandoned building. "We can go out the back of this building, and it will take us to the street with the hospital."

The two entered the building through the broken front window.

"I thought we might need this," she said, pulling a flashlight out of her backpack. Rick smiled.

The two made their way through the building.

"Hey, who are you?" They heard a voice from the dark.

Kate flashed the light in the direction of the voice. There was a man in the corner of the room, it looked as though he had been sleeping there.

"We are just passing through," Rick told the man while continuing to walk.

"You got any food?" the man replied as he started to follow them.

"We are looking for some food ourselves, so no, we don't have anything." Rick just kept moving forward.

The man ran up behind Kate and grabbed her arm to pull her around. Rick turned and stepped back and punched the man square on the jaw. The man fell back. Rick grabbed Kate's hand, and they ran toward the back of the building and stopped and looked back. The man did not follow.

They looked at each other. "You OK?" Rick asked. Kate nodded yes.

The back door to the building was slightly off its hinges. Rick pulled it open. He looked out; the street was clear.

"The hospital should only be a couple blocks down." Kate put the flashlight back in her backpack.

Keeping close to the buildings, they made their way down to the hospital. They could see the glow of the barrel fire as they passed by the intersection just before the hospital.

"Wait." Rick put his arm back to stop Kate. "We will be less likely to be spotted if we cross the street one at a time. You are first." Rick motioned for her to quickly cross.

Kate swiftly crossed and then Rick. They stopped for a moment and listened. It seemed no one saw them, so they continued on. When they reached the hospital front entrance, the windows were broken, and the doors were totally ripped off their hinges.

They stepped through the broken glass. "This way, Rick. This leads down to the pharmacy." Kate again pulled out her flashlight and headed down the hallway.

Items were tossed all over the hall, the rooms were gone through, and the smell was terrible. Kate found a med cart turned upside down in the hallway.

"These drawers are locked. Maybe no one got to the medications." Rick helped Kate pick up the cart and put it back on its wheels.

The cart looked as though it had been beat with a hammer. Two of the drawers were still locked. Kate retrieved her keys from her pocket. She unlocked both drawers. "Anything could be in here," Kate said, looking through the drawer.

Rick removed the backpack from Kate. "We don't have time to sort." Rick started just grabbing the contents and putting it in the backpack.

When they finished with the cart, they continued down to the pharmacy. They needed to work quickly; time was running out before dawn. When they arrived at the pharmacy, it was totally destroyed.

"Let's not waste our time in here. Where to next?" he asked Kate.

"Central supply." She headed for the stairwell. "It's up one floor."

They went up the stairs to the second floor; the door was closed. Rick looked through the small window in the door; he saw no one and opened the door. "Down this way." Kate saw that the door to central supply was open; they entered. Shelves were overturned, and there were a few boxes of bandages and bottles of sterile water on the floor. Other than that nothing was on the shelves. Most of the locked cabinets were opened, but there was one not yet opened. "This cabinet has surgical supplies. We can really use anything we find in here." Kate unlocked the door, and the two just started grabbing anything they could get their hands on and put it in the backpack.

"We are out of time. Let's get out of here." They grabbed the rest of the supplies and headed downstairs. Once on the first floor, they headed back to the front entrance. "We can't go the way we came. That man might still be in that building we came through. We are going to have to take the streets." Rick started to put the backpack on.

"Rick, it will be hard to get behind you on the horse with you carrying the backpack." Rick helped Kate put the pack on and took her hand.

"Ready?" She nodded.

He knew they would have to go farther down the street to avoid the men around the burning barrel. They crossed the street and stuck close to the buildings. When they came to a street crossing, they would quickly go across one at a time, Kate first. They were getting close to the edge of town; Kate went across the last intersection.

"Hey! Who's there?" Kate stopped.

"Keep going," Rick said.

He came into the street. "Stop, I see you there!" Rick stopped as Kate hid behind a dumpster. Rick raised his hands over his head.

"I am unarmed!" he shouted at the man, even though he had a gun under his sweatshirt.

The man approached him, pointing his weapon at Rick. "Why are you out past curfew?"

"I figured it was close enough to daybreak," Rick answered.

"I thought I saw someone else with you," the man questioned.

"No, must have just saw my shadow," Rick replied.

As they spoke another man approached.

"Hey, Mike, what's going on?" the man asked.

"This guy is out past curfew, and I think he has someone with him. Can you look around while I hold him here?"

The man detained Rick while the other man started to search. He started walking toward the dumpster. Kate, hidden behind the dumpster, heard the man approaching, so she picked up a rock and threw across the street, hitting a window. Both men looked toward the window. Rick took his opportunity to grab the guy's gun. The two wrestled for control. Kate took advantage of the distraction and ran toward the edge of town. The other man could not get a clear shot at Rick and started running toward him. The gun went off.

Kate heard the shot and stopped. She waited and closed her eyes. "Please don't let it be Rick," she pleaded. She heard another shot and then saw Rick running toward her.

"Run for the horse!" he shouted.

Kate turned and ran as fast as she could, arriving at the horse and untying it as fast as her fingers could manage. Rick came up beside her and jumped on the horse. Kate reached out her hand, and Rick pulled her up onto the horse, and they took off. Rick could just barely see as the sun was just starting to rise. Kate could hardly hold on to Rick as they ran through the woods along the river. She could hear the sound of a horse following them.

"Rick, it sounds like someone is right behind us!" she shouted.

He tried to quicken the horse's pace. "Hold tight!" he said as he then turned sharply toward the river. He knew there was a good place to cross the river here and quickly crossed and turned back upriver, hoping to confuse the following rider. The rider also crossed but turned downriver and continued his chase in the wrong direction. Rick stopped the horse and waited. He then went back and crossed back over to the other side of the river. "We will see if he turns around." He rode over to shelter themselves behind a group of trees. They waited there quietly.

"I hear someone," Kate whispered. They saw the rider coming back up the other side of the river. He passed them and continued upriver. When he was out of their sights, Rick continued down along the river and back to the farm. After riding for a while, Kate asked, "What happened, Rick?"

"While struggling to get the gun, it went off and shot the man. I grabbed the gun and shot the other man. The men there heard the gunshots and were coming, so I took off running," Rick replied.

Kate sighed and leaned up against Rick. She pulled her hood up over her head to hide herself. "Let's just try to get home as soon as we can." Rick once again quickened the horse's pace; the sun was rising, and they needed to get home.

*****

Back at the farm, Will was starting to get worried that something had gone wrong. The sun was coming up, and Rick and Kate still had not returned. Part of him wanted to saddle up and go look for them, but he knew he needed to stay. Sara was here and still asleep. His thoughts wandered: What if they did not return? How would he manage the farm on his own? What would he do without the both of them? Then he heard the horse whinny. He looked out the window and saw them entering the barn. Will ran down to the barn, opened the door, and saw Kate. He picked her up and swung her around.

"Oh my god, I was so afraid you wouldn't make it back!" Kate pulled down her hood and smiled.

Rick took the saddle off the horse. "We had a close call, but we made it back with supplies. But we will not be doing that again!"

Kate put her hand on Rick's shoulder. "I thought we made a great team."

He took her hand. "Yes, we do make a great team, but let's keep our teamwork at home." Rick kissed Kate on the cheek. She smiled and nodded and took her backpack off and went up to the house and then up the stairs to her room and just fell into bed; the night had been exhausting.

CHAPTER TWELVE

THE SIEGE

KATE HAD SLEPT A FEW hours and was awoken by the sound of the warning bell from the barn. She sat up; she thought maybe she was dreaming, but she heard the bell again. She quickly went downstairs. Sara was in the kitchen.

"Aunt Kate, I was coming to get you. I wasn't sure if you heard the bell."

"Yes, I did. Let's get down to the basement." She led Sara down the stairs and shut and locked the door behind them. "Sara, do you know what is going on?"

"No, I don't. I just was in the kitchen and heard the bell ringing," Sara replied.

Down at the barn, Rick was ringing the bell as Will was running toward the house. They had seen four men approaching from the west pasture on horseback. As the men came closer, Rick recognized one as being in Jefferson last night. He went inside the barn and closed and locked the door. Will arrived at the back porch and went inside. He quickly went to the basement to inform Kate of the approaching men and returned upstairs, grabbed the shotgun, and went back out on the porch. By then the men had arrived at the barn and dismounted from their horses. He could see that Rick had locked himself inside the barn; the men could not open the barn door. Why would Rick not greet them to see what they wanted? Something was wrong. Three of the men remounted their horses and were now riding toward the house; one man stayed behind. Will remained on the porch with his shotgun raised.

"That is far enough," Will stated, aiming the shotgun in the direction of the three men. "Who are you, and what do you want?" he asked.

"Hey, we just want to ask a couple of questions," one of the men said, raising his hands in the air.

"Go ahead," Will said but not lowering his weapon.

"We are looking for a horse with two riders. They were seen in Jefferson last night. Have you seen anyone?" The man stepped closer to the fence.

"No," Will answered. "I would appreciate it if you fellas would move on."

"Seems he is not too friendly, 'fellas,'" the man said, looking over at the others and laughing. "We were admiring your setup here. Looks like you have plenty of food and good water. Not right for you not to share with others. We have been given the authority to take whatever we feel will help our community."

"By whose authority?" Will asked.

"By Mr. Rifle," the man said while taking a shot as Will turned and just made it into the house. The men laughed.

Rick heard the shot; he had been staying out of view from the man walking around the barn, looking for a way in and trying to see inside. Rick looked through a knothole in the barn. He could see the man grabbing his gun from his horse. Rick quietly picked up his rifle. The man took off toward the house. He was confused. Should he leave the barn and go to the house or stay and protect the animals in the barn? They depended on them for survival. He decided he needed to trust Will and Kate and all that they did to protect the house and garden, so he remained locked in the barn.

Will made it in the back door as the bullet flew by his head. He locked the door and went to the window. He opened the window and stuck his shotgun through the opening. "Once again I would appreciate it if you fellas would move on."

The tall man nodded at the others as they split up and surrounded the house. At that point Kate emerged from the basement.

"I heard shots. Thought you might need help." Kate was loading her handgun.

"Yes, Rick is down at the barn, and there are three men surrounding the house," Will answered.

Kate went around to the front of the house and peeked through the curtains. She saw a man standing on the front porch. He had his gun drawn. She watched as he approached the front door and tried to open it. He started kicking the door. Kate opened the window just enough to put her gun through and took a shot in the general direction of the man. He took off running. Kate remained at the window just watching. Her heart was pounding, and she was trying to keep her hands steady. Will had gone over to the side door, where another man was trying to get in by shooting at the lock. Will pushed over the bookcase that was up against the wall to block the door.

Down at the barn, Rick could hear the gunshots. He decided to sneak out of the barn and go up to the house. The animals were important but not as important as the lives of his family. He slowly opened the barn door and looked out. No one was around; the man had gone up to the house. He slipped out the door and put the paddle lock on the barn door. Rick started for the orchard, where he could stay hidden but could observe the house and the intruders. He could see three of the four men; one was at the back of the house on the porch. Two others were walking toward the front. He assumed the other man was on the far side of the house, out of his view. It was late afternoon; the sun was still up for a couple more hours. He thought if he could make it to the pump house, he could take cover there and be within shooting range of the house.

Down in the basement, Sara was listening. She could hear footsteps and gunfire. She knew that she must remain in the basement, but she so wanted to know what was happening upstairs. Was her father all right? Was Aunt Kate? Maybe she could just go to the top of the stairs and peek through the door? No, she told herself; she knew that the safety rules were for her to remain downstairs until she got the all clear. She sat down and put her head in her hands and sighed. Again, she heard footsteps run across the floor and another gunshot. She closed her eyes;

she was scared. She had to believe everything was going to be all right.

Upstairs both Kate and Will heard a window being broken out on the south side of the house. "I know you are in there! You are going to have to come out sooner or later," they heard a man yell through the window.

Will came to Kate. He put his hand to his lips and whispered, "They still do not know you are in here. You stay here in the front of the house, and I will go to the south side of the house." They heard gunfire. "That came from a distance, not from near the house," Will determined.

"It must be Rick," Kate whispered.

Will went over to the south side of the house; he spotted the broken window. He carefully advanced. He did not see a weapon or anyone standing in view. He slowly came up to the side of the window and looked out. He saw a body of a man lying on the ground outside the house. He had been shot. Maybe Kate was right, and Rick had snuck out of the barn and was watching the house. A small amount of relief washed over Will knowing that now he had Rick's help. At this point he needed all the help he could get; it seemed they were outnumbered. Will took another look out the window and saw three men. One was turning over the body of the man on the ground. He could barely hear their conversation.

"That shot did not come from the house. There is someone else out here." The man stood up after examining the body. "We need to take cover."

"It would have had to come from that direction." One of the men pointed over in the direction of the greenhouse.

"I think we should take cover until it gets dark. That would make us less of a target." The tall man headed off to the west side of the house with the others following.

Rick watched as the men took off into the woods. He wasn't sure if they had given up or were just taking cover. He thought if he could get to the back of the house around the garden, he could climb the big oak in the backyard up to the second floor window and get into the house. He figured this was the best time while the men were running for the woods; he might go unnoticed. He looked up. The coast was clear, so he ran for the backyard around the garden. He stopped behind the big oak tree. He looked up and started to climb up the tree. He reached one of the upstairs windows and opened it and climbed inside.

Downstairs Kate looked up toward the ceiling. "It sounds like someone is upstairs." She looked over at Will. He started up the stairs, gun drawn. He slowly went down the hall, then suddenly Rick came through the doorway of the bedroom into the hall.

"It's me! It's me, Rick!" Rick shouted, putting up his hands.

"Holy crap, Rick! I almost shot you!" Will said, putting his gun down. "But boy, I am glad to see you." Will wrapped his arm around Rick's shoulders. "Then that was you that shot the guy. Thought so." The two men went back downstairs, where Kate was waiting.

"Rick!" Kate shouted as she ran and jumped into his arms. "I was afraid they might have shot you."

"Well, I'm here and in one piece." He smiled.

Rick told Will and Kate that the men had ran for the woods, and he expected that they would wait for nightfall to come back. They needed to come up with a plan.

"How about you and I, Will, cover downstairs, and Kate you can cover upstairs? I think that is the safest option for Kate." The three agreed on the plan.

"I am going to check on Sara. She has been downstairs all this time and must be frightened and wondering what is going on."

Will sat down his weapon and went down to the basement. Kate went upstairs into her room. She sat down on the bed. She just started to cry; the stress of everything was getting to her, and she did not want anyone to see her upset. She needed to be strong; this was no time for crybabies. She dried her tears, stood up, and went to peek through the window curtain. It was starting to get dark. She needed to steady herself. Things would only get more intense as the evening progressed. She grabbed a sweater from the closet and put it on and sat in the chair next to the window. Rick walked through the doorway.

"You all right, Kate?" he asked, kneeling down beside her chair.

"I am just peachy," Kate answered.

"Sounds a bit sarcastic to me," he replied as he stood up.

Kate just looked up at him and smiled. "Oh, you know me so well."

Down in the basement, Will was reassuring Sara that everything would be OK, even though he knew there was a good chance it would not. He grabbed a couple of apples from the root cellar and tossed one to Sara. They sat there together, quietly eating their apples.

Sara broke the silence. "Dad, can't I come upstairs and help you? I feel alone down here."

Will shook his head no. "Sara, you are much safer down here in the basement. I want to be able to concentrate upstairs, and if I am so worried about you, I might miss something. I need you safe down here, OK?"

Sara put her head down. "OK, you guys get to have all the fun."

Will laughed. "Not sure I like your idea of fun!" He smiled and turned to go back up the stairs.

As Will returned to the kitchen, Rick had come down from upstairs. He nodded at Will as he headed for the living room to watch the front of the house. Will remained in the kitchen. All was quiet, maybe too quiet. At this time the sun had set, and it was dark out. Rick turned the outside lights on, which he had hooked up to the solar battery. He was hoping that they would last till morning; they needed the lights to keep track of any intruders. He had the curtain open just enough to see outside but able to remain out of view. They kept the lights inside the house turned off so that seeing inside was more difficult. Kate opened the window so she could hear any movement outside. She knew that she needed to also keep an eye on the old oak for any climbers.

*****

The night progressed with no sightings of the men. Will was starting to doze off in the kitchen when Rick walked in and nudged him.

"Hey, wake up!"

Will lifted his head. "Just resting."

Rick reached into the cupboard and got himself a glass for a drink of water.

"Do you think that maybe they gave up and left?" Will suggested.

"That would be the perfect scenario but not likely. They know that we have food and water. I do not think they would give up that easily."

Rick finished his glass of water and started back to the living room. There was the sound of breaking glass and then a scream. Rick ran up the stairs to Kate; Will took off downstairs to the basement. When he arrived at the basement door, there was smoke billowing from under the door. He opened the door.

"Sara!" Will spotted her across the room, which was now of fire. He grabbed a blanket from the cot and tried to throw it over the fire. It was just enough for him to grab Sara. "Are you OK?"

Sara nodded, coughing. "I think so."

Will put her down. "Get upstairs!" he shouted. He went to the sink, looked under it, and found a bucket and filled it with water. At that point Rick arrived; he had brought the fire extinguisher from upstairs and started to help Will put out the fire.

Kate was in the kitchen when Sara reached upstairs. She ran to Kate. "Someone broke the small window in the basement and threw in something that was on fire," she explained while still coughing from the smoke.

Kate took Sara over to the kitchen sink, got her a drink of water, and washed her face with a wet dishcloth. "Better?" she asked. Sara nodded. Kate heard footsteps run across the back porch. She pushed Sara behind her. She saw a couple of shadows pass the porch light heading to the back door. Kate pushed Sara toward the table. "Sara, get under the kitchen table." Sara slid under the table. Kate reached for her weapon as she went and stood to the side of the door. She could hear the men whispering.

Rick and Will had managed to get the fire out. "Looks like it did not do too much damage," Rick stated while putting down his fire extinguisher.

"Someone threw a burning bottle of whiskey through the window." Will observed while picking up the whiskey bottle from the scorched floor.

Both men turned their heads to the basement door when they heard a shotgun blast from upstairs. Both ran for the stairs. When they reached the kitchen, they saw where the men had blown a big hole in the back door with a shotgun. The men were attempting to climb through the hole in the door. Kate had been knocked down from the blast and scrambling to pick up her gun. Will had his gun and shot at the men attempting to climb in the door. He hit the man in the front. The other men started returning fire. Rick had gone over to Kate to assist her out of the doorway. He grabbed her and pulled her to the side, then picked up her gun.

Will yelled at Sara, "Go upstairs and take cover!"

Sara flew up the stairs and hid in the linen closet. Rick and Will knocked over the large kitchen table and took cover. Kate remained on the floor, keeping herself up against the wall.

"There was three of them. One has been shot. Two remain." Rick ran out of ammunition. "I've got to get to my rifle." He had left it on the counter when he picked up the fire extinguisher. Kate saw the rifle on the counter and crawled along the cabinets till she could reach up and grab the gun. She slid it across the floor to Rick.

"Here, Rick." Rick picked up the gun and started returning fire. Finally, the two men retreated into the woods, and the gunfire stopped.

"We can't let them get away. They will tell others and bring back reinforcements," Will said, loading another magazine into his weapon.

"What are you saying? That we should kill them?" Rick asked.

"What choice do we have? They are trying to kill us, take our home, and God knows what they would do with Kate and Sara! I am going after them." Will ran out the door after the men. Rick knew Will was right. He looked over at Kate.

"What are you waiting for, Rick? Go! I can handle things here. I've got the shotgun," Kate said, waving Rick off. He ran off in the direction of the men.

Kate went upstairs to find Sara. She called for her, and she came out of the linen closet, where she was hiding. Kate took Sara's hand and led her to her bedroom, shut the door, and slid the dresser over against the door.

Sara looked over at Kate. "Aunt Kate, I'm afraid. I don't like all this fighting!"

Kate walked up to Sara and put her hands on her shoulders. "I'm afraid too, Sara. All we can do is just keep trying to survive and hope for moments of happiness." Kate knew that was not too encouraging, but it was the truth.

Rick caught up with Will. "Do you know what direction they headed?" he asked.

"Their horses are grazing up over there"—Will pointed at the men's horses—"so they must still be around. I saw movement down by the barn."

Rick looked toward the barn. "If we stay hidden near the horses, maybe we can wait them out. They are going to have to go for the horses at some point. It is a long ride back to Jefferson."

Rick and Will quickly found a place near the horses where they could watch for the men and see the barn. They finally saw the men. They were trying to get into the barn. Rick had paddle locked the door. Will took a shot at the men. He could see one go down. The other man took cover behind the barn. The man on the ground was crawling to try to make it to the water trough.

"Now that one is injured, they definitely will need the horses." Rick quickly went over to the horses, grabbed the reins of two, and scared off the other two. The man behind the barn took a shot at Rick; it grazed his arm. He led the two horses into the woods.

"Rick, are you OK?" Will asked, grabbing one of the horses.

"Yeah, it just grazed me."

"Can you still ride and shoot? It's harder to hit a moving target," Will asked while jumping up on the horse.

Rick mounted his horse, and off they both went toward the barn, Will to the left and Rick to the right. Rick saw the man behind the barn running toward the trees. He took a shot, and the man dropped. Will found the man behind the water trough, but he was already dead. Rick rode to the man and jumped off his horse, aiming his gun at his head.

"You have a woman in the house, don't you?" asked the man, grasping for air and blood running from his mouth.

"Yes, my wife," Rick answered, "but how did you know?"

"Because if I had a woman, I would do anything to protect her, and you obviously risked your life for her." The man closed his eyes and was gone. Rick stood there for a moment, then went and picked up the man's gun. "You're damn right I would risk my life for her, you asshole."

CHAPTER THIRTEEN

THE PROPOSAL

BEFORE WINTER SET IN, RICK wanted to make another trip to Jefferson. They needed to restock some of their supplies.

Certain items had been getting harder to obtain, requiring creative solutions. They had been growing sugarcane in the greenhouse, which Rick had gotten from a neighbor before things turned desperate. They knew it would now be great for trading.

Kate prepared some sugarcane, jars of fruit, and corn for trading, then packed some boiled eggs and apples for Rick to eat on his trip.

"I should be back tomorrow," Rick said. Then he added with a smirk, "Try not to let any tree branches come through your window."

Kate thought, *what a smart-ass remark,* but instead just smiled and said, "Be safe and come home in one piece."

Rick tipped his hat to her and went out the door to pack the horses. He had decided to ride along the river to stay off the road, where he would be more likely to run into trouble. He had his rifle in the saddle beside him and his handgun in his jacket pocket.

After he had ridden for several hours, he stopped to let the horse drink from the river. He was reaching in his saddlebag to get an apple when he heard a noise coming from the woods. He seized his rifle and aimed it at the sound. He listened but heard only the river. After a while he put his rifle back and returned to his apple. When he finished, he went to his horse and continued his journey.

While he was riding, out of the corner of his eye, he saw something moving, as though it was following him. He slowed his horse, then stopped. He scanned the other side of the river, certain he had seen something moving. He continued, and again he noticed something moving.

Back at the farm, Will came in from outside and went down to the basement, where Kate was helping Sara with her sewing.

"Hey, Kate," Will interrupted, "can I talk to you a moment upstairs?"

"OK, just a minute," Kate replied, feeling odd about both the question and her answer, before Will turned and went back up the stairs. Turning to Sara, she said, "Please just continue to work on your seams. I'll be back."

When Kate entered the kitchen, Will grabbed her and swung her around.

"Finally, alone!" he exclaimed, kissing her and feeling her return the passion. "There are times I look at you and just want to grab and hold on to you," he whispered in her ear.

Kate loved Will's passion and playfulness, but she also felt a growing amount of guilt and, with it, resistance to impede on the love she still had for Rick.

"Will, do you think it's possible to love two people at the same time?" she asked, then felt self-conscious about what she had asked.

"That's an odd question," Will said as he looked puzzled at Kate.

"No, really, it's not. I am in love with you." Will smiled. "But I still love Rick," Kate countered, causing Will to step back from her. "I love you both for different reasons." She sat down and hung down her head.

Will sat down beside her and lifted her chin.

"Kate," he replied calmly, "there are so many kinds of love. You can love your spouse but not the same as you love your child. You love your mother but not the same as you love your best friend. So yes, you can love two people at the same time."

"Yes," Kate insisted, "but what about being in love with two men at the same time?"

At that point Sara came up from the basement and, before she could say anything, looked at Kate and Will.

"Did I interrupt something?" Sara asked.

"We were just talking," Kate answered. "Did you already finish?"

"No, I need your help again," Sara answered.

"Very good," Kate replied. "I'll meet you back downstairs." Kate rose to follow Sara and turned to Will.

"How about we continue our conversation later?" Will asked as he winked at her. Kate smiled quickly and left the room.

*****

When Rick arrived in Jefferson, he saw it had grown in size since his last visit. There were more men trading goods as well as more tension in the air. More of the buildings had broken windows, and some had been burned to the ground. A man crossed his horse's path. "Hey, you got any food?" Rick just casually touched his rifle; the man moved on. He saw a crowd at the end of the street, gathered around a man up on a small stage. He rode down the street to see what the gathering was all about.

"The reward for women has gone up," the man said. "I am offering goods like food, seeds for planting, livestock, and even gas for your automobiles." The man paused for effect. He was tall, well-dressed, clean-shaven, and well-spoken.

"There is no more valuable item around. I'm offering rewards for information regarding the whereabouts of women or for their capture but only if they are captured alive."

Rick felt sick to his stomach. He stood there listening to gauge the crowd's sentiments.

"How about we get together and organize some search parties?" one man proposed.

Another offered, "I heard there were women hiding up in the mountains to the east."

All Rick could think was to get back home to Kate, and the sooner he could trade his goods, the better.

*****

Dusk was settling on the farm. Will was putting the horses in the barn and checking on the steer as Kate and Sara were cooking. It was getting cooler outside, so Kate had started a fire in the woodstove in the living room.

"That feels nice," Will said as he came in the house, "and something smells good too."

Kate had made some bread from the last of the flour, and Will tried to grab a piece.

"Hey, you go wash up first," Kate said, slapping his hand and laughing.

Kate and Sara set the table, and the three sat down. They enjoyed dinner and decided to play cards after the dishes were done.

Sara hated losing, and Will would call her out for cheating every time she won.

"Well, Dad, you have to cheat to beat me!" she retorted with a smile.

"Well, you both have to cheat to beat me!" Kate laughed.

They played cards into the night until Sara could not stop yawning.

"Young lady, you should go off to bed," Will told Sara. "It is getting late."

"No! I want to play another game!" Sara said defiantly. Will just gave her that Dad look.

"OK, Dad," Sara said as she kissed Will then Kate good night and went upstairs.

"Kate, you just don't know what a good influence you have been on Sara. She has become much better behaved. I think you have had a lot to do with that."

Will got up and took Kate's hand.

"Let's go sit by the fire," he proposed.

They went to the living room and sat next to each other on the couch, where they sat quietly for a while, Kate with her head on Will's shoulder watching the fire and Will holding her hand.

Will looked into Kate's eyes and said, "I have fallen in love with you, Kate."

Kate smiled and replied, "I love you too."

"I have been thinking about our situation all afternoon. I know we both are having feelings of guilt regarding Rick," Will declared. "I have decided to ask Rick if he would share you."

"What!" Kate admonished. "You're out of your mind!"

"Shhh," Will whispered, "you will wake up Sara. And no, I am not out of my mind. I don't want you to think that I'm in love with you because you're the only woman around. I had no intentions of falling in love with you. It just happened. But Rick is my brother, and I don't want to go behind his back."

"I don't want to go behind his back either," Kate continued, "but there's no way Rick would be inclined to such an arrangement." Her head was spinning.

"I feel it is the best solution to a difficult problem and really our only option," Will interjected.

"Explain to me exactly what you mean by 'share.' Do you mean like open marriage or polyandry?" Kate raised her eyebrows.

"That is exactly what I mean, like you having two husbands or partners. It seems due to our circumstances, that being there are way more men on the planet than woman, should increase the odds of Rick possibly accepting such an arrangement, some form of polyandry or double marriage. Sex ratios are becoming highly uneven, which is not a problem we anticipated. A woman will need to be paired up with multiple partners to improve the chance of survival of the human race. It would be to Rick's advantage. When he is absent, I am here to protect you and our home. Rick and I have different strengths, points of view, and styles, which put together make for a better support system for you. I have no problem with Rick being the so-called 'first husband.' He has been with you and loved you for many years. I just want to be part of your life as your friend, lover, and protector." Will ended with a kiss.

Kate had listened intently to Will's explanation. "You make some good points, but this will be challenging for Rick to understand, what we are asking him to do. Out of love and respect for him, this has to be his decision, and we will have to accept what he decides. And he would have to be the one to make the ground rules, which there will be many, I'm sure." She continued, "Will, if we do this, it has to be asked in a very careful way, at the right time." Kate put her head on Will's chest and sighed.

Will agreed, "It is a strange and delicate situation. Good timing is essential."

*****

Rick successfully traded all his goods, even got some coffee, which he knew Kate would be excited about. He packed up his supplies and started for home, following the river for a few miles before making camp for the night. It was a cold night, so he made a fire. As he sat by the fire eating the boiled eggs from his saddlebag, again he heard a noise coming from the darkness. He put his hand on his rifle.

"Who's there?" he called out, standing up and aiming his rifle in the direction of the sound. "Come out!" he shouted.

Out of the dark came a dog, with its head down and tail wagging.

"Well, hello there," Rick relented, putting down his rifle and approaching the dog. "You look pretty hungry there, girl."

He reached down slowly to pet the dog. She came closer to smell him, then wagged her tail. She was a medium-sized dog, with a mostly white coat mixed with some brown patches and a patch covering one eye. Rick reached in his saddlebag and pulled out a couple of eggs.

"Here, girl, have one of these," Rick offered and tossed toward the pup, who inhaled it. He tossed her another egg, which she also inhaled.

He sat down next to the fire, and the pooch came up and sat down beside him.

"So you're the one who has been following me all day," Rick welcomed. "I think I even remember seeing you in Jefferson. I have to admire your moxie." He thought for a moment. "Hey, that's a great name for you,

Moxie! So yes, I guess you can hang out with me around the fire tonight."

The two fell asleep next to the fire until Rick was awoken early in the morning by Moxie growling. Dawn was just breaking. Rick grabbed his rifle and looked around.

"What is it, girl?"

Moxie again growled, then started barking. Among the trees in the direction of her barking, Rick saw a mountain lion. Rick took a shot in the general direction of the cat, and it ran off into the woods.

"Well, Moxie, it looks like I owe you one," he said as he bent down and patted the dog. "Let's go home," he said, packing up his things, and him and Moxie started out for home.

Will and Kate had fallen asleep together on the couch beside the fire. They were awoken by the sound of a dog barking.

"Is that a dog?" Will said, getting up to look out the window.

"It sure sounds like it," Kate agreed.

As he looked, Will saw Rick had returned home and that a dog was following him and his horse to the barn.

"Rick is back," Will said, "and he has a dog."

"A dog, now that's strange," Kate reflected as she went to the window to peek out. "Rick never wanted a dog." She saw the dog trailing behind Rick. "I guess we will get the story when he comes up to the house."

Will stepped away from the window.

"So we have decided to tell Rick about our little situation, right?" he asked.

"I think that is our only choice, to explain our situation and see what he says," Kate sighed. "To continue going behind his back is only asking for trouble."

Will put his arms around Kate's waist.

"I agree, but like you suggested, it will need to be a good time to ask."

Kate looked at Will, then smirked before stealing a quick kiss.

"There will never be a good time."

Rick walked in through the back door, and Kate walked up and hugged him.

"I'm glad you're home," she said as she bent down to pat the dog. "Who is your new friend?"

Moxie licked Kate right across the face.

"Well, looks like she likes you." Rick laughed. "This is Moxie. We met along the way to Jefferson."

Rick set down the box of supplies he got in Jefferson on the table. Rick told them the story of how he met Moxie, and they all agreed she would make a fine addition to the family.

"Sara will love her," Will added.

As Kate went through the new supplies and put them away, Rick nodded at Will to follow him into the living room and told him about the man offering goods as a reward for information about or the capture of women. Will sat down and shook his head.

"We have to do all we can do to protect Sara and Kate," he declared. "I love them both and couldn't take it if anything happened to either of them."

Rick put his hand on Will's shoulder.

"I'm with you, brother."

CHAPTER FOURTEEN

TILL DEATH DO US PART

THE MORNING SUN BROUGHT WARMTH to the air but not enough to subdue the cold breeze that was blowing. Rick was bringing in more wood from outside and placing it in the woodbin, while Will was making coffee, and Kate was making her way down the stairs to the kitchen.

"Good morning, Will," Kate said as Will handed her a cup of coffee. "Oh, you are an angel," she said while taking a sip of the coffee.

"Well, I can't take all the credit. It was Rick that was able to trade for it, but I will take the compliment," Will replied, then paused before continuing. "So is today a good day for our discussion with Rick?"

"It's as good as any," she replied. "Let's just rip off the Band-Aid."

"I always enjoy your metaphors." Will laughed.

Rick entered the kitchen, and Will poured him some coffee.

"Now that smells so good." Rick smelled and sipped the coffee.

"Rick," he cut in, "can Kate and I talk to you before you head back outside?"

Rick took another sip of his coffee.

"Sure, what's up?"

Kate felt a knot in her stomach and looked over at Will, needing him to have the strength to continue.

"I'll start," Will said. "Let's sit down."

Will sat at the kitchen table, and Rick and Kate followed.

"I am sure you can see that I have become very close with Kate," Will began nervously. "Living in the situation we are currently in, it is understandable that both of us would come to love one another. The world has changed, and we have had to adapt to those changes."

Rick sipped his coffee again.

"Get to the point. You not making any sense," he directed.

Kate stood up and blurted, "Will and I want to know if you will share."

"Share what?" Rick asked, puzzled.

"Me," Kate answered.

Rick looked at Kate and replied, still perplexed, "I'm sorry, but I don't understand what you are asking."

"It's like this," Will interjected, standing up. "The chances of me finding a woman to love and be with in this crazy world are zero. We were wondering if you would share Kate with me in every way. I'm not sure I could ask any more plainly."

Rick was silent at first, then he stood and looked down at Will. "You are asking me to share my wife. In what way are we talking about?"

"In every way. I guess the best way to put it would be as if I was also her husband, with the same privileges," Will said, squirming in his chair.

"So basically you're asking if you can have sex with my wife," Rick confronted him.

"Rick, it's more than that," Will contended.

Rick's face went red.

"No," he stammered, "I think that's all it is about."

"I love her, Rick," Will countered.

"I can't believe my brother just asked me to share my wife. I should punch you in the face." Rick stood there with his fist clenched.

Rick walked toward the back door and, just before opening it, looked back right at Will.

"I need to talk alone to my wife about this. Can we have some privacy?" Rick asked as he walked back over to Kate. Will nodded and went down to the basement. Rick grabbed Kate's hand and led her to the kitchen table, then sat her down and looked her in the eyes.

"Are you OK with this?" he asked.

Kate looked back at Rick.

"Yes, Rick, I love you both," she cajoled. "The world has changed. It would be almost impossible for Will to find another woman. Besides, we have grown to love each other very much. And my love for you has not diminished. There is room for both of you in my heart. The circumstance of our lives has changed. I am not saying there wouldn't be adjustments. There are pros and cons to accepting this change in our lifestyle. You know you could always rely on Will to protect me and the farm, relieving you of some of the responsibility."

"Is this because I have not given you enough attention? Do you think I do not desire you anymore? Will has expressed to me that I do not give you enough time and affection. Is that what you think?" Rick countered.

"There has been a lack of affection, but I do not think it is because you do not love me. I believe that you are so wrapped up in survival and protecting me that some of my basic needs have not been met. I do not blame you. Life has become difficult, and I so appreciate everything you do to keep us alive and fed. Our lives have become very stressful, and we just must make the best of it. I will abide by whatever you decide. The choice is yours." Kate knew it would be hard for Rick to understand how she felt, and she expressed herself the best she could. Now it was up to him.

Rick got up from the table and went back toward the door and walked out, leaving Kate sitting there alone. Will came back up from the basement.

"I heard the door slam, "Will stated. "Why didn't he yell or scream and punch me in the face like he said?" Will went to the window and looked out. "He's just standing there in the middle of the yard." Will came and sat beside Kate.

"Let's just let him think about it," she said. "We need to give him some time. This was a totally unexpected surprise and is a lot to process."

"OK," Will agreed. "I am going to check on Sara."

Will went upstairs to Sara's room, where she was playing with the new dog.

"You sure are enjoying that new pup, aren't you?" Will smiled.

"I love her!" Sara beamed.

"Well, I'm sorry to interrupt," Will replied, "but she needs to go outside for a while, and you have some chores to do."

Will whistled for Moxie to follow him outside and out to the barn. Rick caught sight of Will and stopped him at the barn door.

Will opened the door to the barn and went in. Rick followed and shut the door behind him.

"Have you two already been together?" Rick's eyes burned.

Will knew he could never tell Rick the truth.

"No, we didn't want to go behind your back. That is why we are asking about sharing." Will knew if he didn't lie to Rick, he would never consider his request.

Rick grabbed his horse and saddled her up. "I need to think about this, and the only reason I am even considering this is because you are my brother and I love Kate." He jumped on the horse and rode away.

Will grabbed the milking bucket.

"So, Moxie," Will said, eyeing her, "are you sure you want to get mixed up with this family?"

The dog tilted her head and looked at Will, then wagged her tail.

Kate and Sara were in the basement. Kate was teaching Sara how to churn milk into butter.

"It takes a while for it to turn to butter," Kate explained as she handed Sara the dasher to the churn for herself. Sara grabbed the wooden handle and started to churn.

"Do you think things will ever get back to how they were?" Sara asked.

"No, not like they were before," Kate lamented, "but I do think we will find a way to return to some kind of normalcy."

Sara shrugged at Kate, and the two ladies continued with their butter making.

Will came in with more milk. "Here, ladies, more milk just for you." Will laughed.

Will winked at Kate and motioned her over to him.

"I had to lie to Rick." Will hung down his head.

"He asked you if we had been together, didn't he?" She pulled him further away from Sara.

He nodded. "Yes."

"I understand. You had no choice but to lie. He would never consider our request if he knew. I am sorry he put you in the situation," Kate apologized.

Will looked at her. "He didn't put me in the situation. We put ourselves in that situation."

"Maybe this has been a mistake," Kate admitted.

"Kate, if being with you had been a mistake, it's been a beautiful mistake."

Rick had ridden for about an hour before stopping by the river for some water. Rick tried to picture what exactly sharing his wife actually meant. Protecting her, making sure she had food, water, and shelter, those were all things that Will could help provide and he should, being a member of this family. But sharing her love, her attention, and her affection, that was something else entirely. The thought of Will touching her was a hard one for him to swallow. Rick knew the world had changed. Was it fair that Will would not have the joys of having a woman in his life because of the state of the world? It wasn't as easy as if it was right or wrong anymore. *Maybe adjustments could be made*, he thought. The request to share his wife had come from his own brother, but he wasn't sure if that made it easier or harder to decide. He needed to discuss this more with Will and Kate. This is a decision he could not make lightly. No matter what decision he made, his world had already been turned upside down. He mounted his horse to start home, pulling his coat up around his neck against the bite of the wind.

As Rick grew closer to the farmhouse, he saw a truck driving on the gravel road off in the distance. He thought it was strange to see a vehicle out there, as any gas was in short supply and usually saved for a tractor. It was heading in the direction of their farmhouse. Rick pushed the horse's stirrups.

"Come on, girl," he urged, "we need to get back home fast!"

Will was taking some eggs up to Kate in the kitchen.

"Wait out here on the porch, Moxie," Will told the dog.

He went inside and handed Kate the basket of eggs. He let her know he was going to be outside splitting some wood for the rest of the afternoon. He grabbed his jacket, wrapping his arms around Kate's waist and giving her a kiss before heading back outside.

While chopping wood, he thought about Rick possibly saying yes to his and Kate's request. He hadn't fully thought about what he would tell Sara if he said yes. This was going to be confusing for her but not something that he could keep from her; she would need to know. But how would she accept it? Suddenly, Moxie started barking.

"What is it, Moxie?" Will asked urgently before Moxie pushed by him, running up to the house barking. Will could hear what sounded like a truck coming up the driveway, and he started running up to the front of the house. Moxie was on the front porch, barking and growling. Will arrived up on the porch about the same time an old pickup truck pulled up in front of the house. Two men and a boy were in the front seat of the truck. One man jumped out of the truck and pointed a rifle at Will. Will raised his hands.

"Hey, I am unarmed!" Will pleaded.

The other man came out of the truck and walked up to Will.

"So, where is the woman?" he demanded. "The boy said her name is Kate. And call off your dog." Moxie was pulling at the man's pant leg.

Will put Moxie in the front door of the house, knowing that Moxie's barking would warn Kate and Sara.

"Hey, I'm not sure what you're talking about," Will countered. "There are no women here, just my brother and I."

Kate and Sara heard Moxie barking.

"Something is wrong," Kate said to Sara. The two ran down to the basement. "Get in the armoire," Kate instructed as she locked the door to the basement. She retrieved her handgun and loaded it. She joined Sara in the armoire and shut the door. They listened but could not hear what was going on over the dog's barking. Kate knew something was different, and she knew Will was alone. How long should she wait? How long was Rick going to be gone? She knew someone who did not belong was there. She stuck her head out of the armoire. "I need to be able to hear. Sara, I need to go upstairs and see what is going on," Kate decided. "I want you to stay in the armoire, and here, take the gun. Promise me you'll stay here until I come get you."

"I promise," Sara whispered.

Kate opened the door, climbed out, and went quietly up to the kitchen. Moxie came to her.

"Good girl, Moxie," she said. "Now you go downstairs and protect Sara." She shut the basement door, then went to the front door to listen.

"I'm only going to ask you one more time," the man persisted. "Where is the woman?"

The man waved at the boy in the truck. The boy climbed out, and Will saw it was Pete. Will knew they were screwed.

"She and my brother went for a ride," Will said desperately.

"He is full of shit," said the other man holding the rifle. "She is in the house."

The man walked closer to Will, pulled out a knife, and suddenly grabbed him and held the knife to his throat.

"What do you have to say now?" he threatened.

At that moment Rick rode up behind the truck, slid down from his horse, and came around from behind.

"Drop the knife!" Rick shouted.

The man grabbed Will tighter.

"By the time you shoot, he'll be dead."

Rick walked closer, still aiming the rifle.

Kate moved to just behind the front door and grabbed the shotgun.

"Listen, Kate," the man shouted, "I will have my man shoot your husband! It's as simple as that, unless you come out!"

The man nodded at the other man, who raised his rifle and aimed it directly at Rick's head, his finger on the trigger. Rick turned and aimed his rifle back in return.

"No, Kate, don't come out," Will shouted, "and grab ahold of the shotgun!"

"So are you willing to die for a little pussy?" The man laughed as he dug the knife into Will's cheek.

"I'm getting impatient, Kate!" demanded the man.

Meanwhile, downstairs Sara was waiting in the cabinet. She was worried it had been way too long. She climbed out of the cabinet. Moxie came up to her. "Hi, Moxie, what's going on up there?" Sara went up to the basement door and listened. She could hear voices but could not hear them clearly. "Moxie, you stay down here. I don't need you barking." Sara went up the stairs, taking the gun for protection. She arrived upstairs just as Kate went out the front door. Rick started toward Kate.

"Not so fast," said the man, shooting at Rick's feet.

"I know I'm worth more alive than dead," Kate said, holding the shotgun at her chin. "Let the men go, and I will come with you."

"Kate, *no*!" Will pleaded.

The two men looked at each other.

"You put down your weapon, and we will let them go."

"Do you think I am stupid?" Kate retorted. "You put down your weapons and back away. Rick, you need to put down your rifle also."

Rick laid down his rifle in front of him and backed away, and the other man with a rifle placed his on the ground.

"Well, I'm not stupid either," the man with the knife asserted, keeping the knife on Will's neck.

"OK, this is how this is going to go," Kate asserted as she pointed her gun at the man with the knife. "I'm going to lower my weapon as you let Will go."

"All right." The man nodded. "As long as this guy doesn't try anything stupid."

The man lowered his knife as Kate lowered her gun. He let go of Will as Kate laid her gun on the ground. As Will moved away, the man grabbed Kate and placed the knife to her throat. Rick quickly grabbed his gun.

"Now don't think I won't harm her," the man snarled, "so back off."

At that moment Sara stepped out of the house and onto the porch and aimed her pistol square at the man holding Aunt Kate. The man froze, staring at her, while the other man raised his rifle and aimed it at Uncle Rick.

"Sara, go back inside!" Will shouted.

Rick lifted his rifle and shot the man holding the knife to Kate, and the other man fired immediately and shot Rick. Sara swiveled and shot the man with the rifle. It all happened so fast. Kate ran to Rick; he had been shot straight through his chest. Kate placed her hands over the wound.

"Will, come help me get him to the basement!" Kate shouted desperately.

Rick grabbed her hand. "Kate, it's OK. I know I do not have much time, so please listen." Kate, crying, looked him in the eyes. "Kate, I love you! I will always love you. Take care of yourself, and you have my blessing to be with Will."

Will had ran up to Sara. She was still standing there holding the gun. "It's over, Sara. You did good. Let me have the gun." Will took the gun from her hands. Sara clung on to her father; he hugged her. "It's all going to be OK." Sara looked up at Kate and Rick. Will turned. "Sara, I need to help Aunt Kate now."

Will ran over to Kate. "Is he OK?" Rick looked over at Will.

"Will, my brother, please look after Kate, I know you love her, and please protect her."

Will looked at his brother. "I will protect her with my life, just as you have done here today."

Rick closed his eyes. Kate kissed him gently on his lips. "I love you too, Rick, and I will forever." She felt for his pulse, but he was gone. She sat there beside him crying.

Will stood up and walked over to Sara. "Let's go inside, Sara. We need to give Aunt Kate a few moments alone."

Sara looked over at Pete still inside the truck. "What about the boy?"

"You go on inside," Will insisted. "I will get the boy."

Will went to the truck.

"Hi, Pete, are you OK?" Will asked.

Pete nodded yes, then, with his eyes lowered, said, "I'm sorry. I didn't want anything like this to happen. Those were very bad men."

Will took Pete's hand and said, "Don't worry, it's over now. Let's go into the house, and I'll introduce you to Sara."

As soon as Sara saw Pete, she was enraged. "He is the boy who told the men about Aunt Kate!"

Will sat Pete at the table.

"Sara, he is just a small boy who was afraid of those men who used him. Look at him. He is frightened just like you."

Sara looked at Pete. He was dirty and smelly and had bruises on his face.

"I did not want to tell!" Pete pleaded, and started crying.

Sara took pity on him and put her arm around him.

"Can I get you a glass of milk?" she offered.

While Sara looked after Pete, Will went back outside, where he found Kate still sitting on the ground next to Rick.

"Will, can you help me get him inside?" she asked, looking up as he came closer.

Will came over and helped Kate lift Rick.

"I want to take him to our room upstairs," she said.

The two proceeded to take Rick in the house and place him on their bed.

"I can take it from here, Will. Thank you," she said, shutting the bedroom door.

Will went back outside to take care of the other two dead bodies. He put the two bodies in the back of their truck, then pulled the truck into the barn and shut the door. He siphoned most of the gas from the truck to use for the tractor. He decided he would wait till dark, then go down to the river and drive the truck out into the water and let it sink.

Kate had gotten a bowl of water and a washcloth and was cleaning Rick's face.

"I will never forget what you did for me," she told him and leaned down to kiss him. "I will always love you."

She looked over at their wedding picture she had on her dresser. What was she going to do now without him?

She went over to the closet and pulled out his best shirt and pants. She finished washing his body and then dressed him and combed his hair. She sat there holding his hand, not wanting to let him go. She heard a knock on the door.

"Aunt Kate, can we come in?" Sara asked.

"Not now," Kate replied, not yet ready to see anyone. "Please go away."

Sara was with Pete. Will came up the stairs behind them.

"Come on, you two," Will said. "I think you both could use some rest."

Will took Pete into his room.

"Here, Pete, you can lie down on my bed," he offered. "You have had a rough day."

Pete crawled up onto Will's bed and closed his eyes. Will went down to Sara's room, where she was looking at a necklace Uncle Rick had given her.

"I will miss him," she said.

"I know it has been a terrible day for you," Will said. "I never asked you about shooting the man. I hope you understand that I don't blame you for what you did. It was a brave thing to do," Will conveyed to Sara.

"Thank you," she said.

"You need to rest," he said. "Lie down and close your eyes."

Will pulled the blanket up around Sara and kissed her on the cheek.

Sara had finally fallen asleep, and Will heard Kate open the door to her bedroom. He walked down the hall to meet her. Kate reached out and hugged him.

"I know you loved him in your own way," Will said as he held her, "and I know he loved you." Will thought for a moment. "What a sacrifice Rick made to keep you alive and here with us."

"I was thinking we can put him next to your parents in the garden," Kate proposed.

"Yes, that sounds good," Will agreed with tears in his eyes. "I'll start building a casket." Will sobbed for a moment. "The world has become a sad, brutal place. It is going to be difficult taking care of this farm with just us," he added after he finished and gave Kate a kiss. "I'm going down to the barn to see what lumber I have."

"What are we going to do with the truck and the other two men?" Kate asked.

"Don't worry," Will said. "I'll take care of it."

Kate hugged Will one more time, walked into the bedroom, and shut the door.

Outside, it was almost dark. Will tied one of the horses to the tailgate of the truck so that he would have a ride back to the farm, then stood there for a moment and looked at the two men in the back of the truck, their faces now oddly peaceful. Will opened the barn door, climbed in the truck, and pulled away while Kate peeked out through the curtain, unseen, to watch the taillights disappear from her bedroom window. Kate looked over at Rick's body still lying on their bed. He had protected her until the end. She wondered if he would still be alive if she had done things differently. They had been together for so many years. It would be strange not having him nearby. Kate went downstairs to the kitchen. She poured herself a glass of milk and sat down at the kitchen table. She could not sleep. The day kept repeating in her mind over and over.

Will had arrived at the river. He stopped, untied the horse, put the truck in neutral, and pushed it off the bank and into the river. He watched the truck sink down to the bottom. "May they burn in hell!" Will climbed up on the horse and started for home. On his ride back, he worried how he was going to manage taking care of the farm and the family on his own. His heart hurt that Rick was gone, but he was also angry at him for leaving him alone to protect Sara and Kate. Among his feelings he was grateful; he saved Kate at his own expense. Sara needed Kate, and he needed her also. When he arrived back at the farm, he returned to his work on Rick's casket. Sara had found one of Grandmother Campbell's quilts and given it to Will. He used it to line the casket.

By the time Will had completed the coffin, it was early in the morning; the sun was just starting to rise. He closed the door and went to the house; he came in the back door into the kitchen. Kate was sitting in a kitchen chair with her head lying on the table. Will walked up quietly; she was asleep. He touched her shoulder. "Kate, Kate."

She raised her head. "What time is it?" she said, rubbing the crick in her neck.

"It's almost 5:00 a.m. Come on up to bed," Will said, encouraging her.

"Rick is still in our bed," she muttered, standing.

"Come lie in my bed. You need some rest." Kate followed Will upstairs and into his room.

"I will go lie down on the couch downstairs." He covered Kate with the blanket. She grabbed his hand.

"Don't go. Please stay here with me." She pulled the blanket back.

He climbed in next to her; she pulled up the blanket. He lay up against her and whispered, "I will protect you with my life, just as my brother did. I want you to know that."

The two fell asleep and woke up later with both Sara and Pete sleeping at the bottom of the bed.

"We will be protecting those two together. I think we have our work cut out for us." Kate got up and woke the children.

"Sara, Pete, time to get up and get dressed. We have a funeral to prepare." Kate left the room and went down the hall.

Sara ran after her. "Wait, Aunt Kate, we have no clothes for Pete."

Will came up beside them. "I think there might be some of my old clothes in the attic. I will take a look."

Later in the morning, everyone had finished their assigned chores and was washed, dressed, and had gathered together. Will laid Rick's body inside the coffin and he, Sara, Kate, and Pete all helped to carry it out to the garden. A grave had already been dug, and they placed the casket inside. They all stood around the grave.

"My dear husband, you protected and loved me till the very end. You will be missed, but there will always be a spot in my heart for you," Kate said with tears in her eyes.

"Dear brother, it saddens me that we just renewed our relationship and you have now been taken from us. Rest at peace knowing that I will protect our family. Love you, my brother."

Will picked up a shovel. Sara grabbed Pete's hand to back him up while her father buried the casket. When he had finished, he placed the grave marker he had carved at the top of the grave. It read, "Rick Campbell, husband, protector, loved, never forgotten." Sara placed a single rose from the garden on his grave while tears run down her face. Will grabbed her hand and Pete's, and the three walked away.

Kate stood there alone for a moment and slowly lowered her head. "Our chapter has ended, Rick, but another has now started for me and the family. Rest peacefully." She turned and walked away.

Will and the children stopped to wait for Kate. "Pete, take Sara's hand." Pete walked over and took ahold of Sara's hand, freeing Will's. Kate walked up, and Will extended his hand to her. She took his hand, and the four of them returned to the old farmhouse. When they entered the house, Sara turned to Pete.

"Now that you are going to be part of our family, you need to learn the safety rules. There are quite a few, but I will teach them all to you. Now follow me. We will start the tour in the basement. That is the safest place in the house." Pete followed Sara to the basement. "Uncle Rick said the rules are for the protection of our family."

ABOUT THE AUTHOR

KAT TAPPAN

KAT WRITES FICTION WITH A lot of drama and a twist of romance (or is it romance with a twist?).

Inspired by her vivid imagination, she began writing her debut novel *For the Protection of a Woman* after a brush with death. Today she is pursuing her dream of being a published novelist in between the demands of a health–care worker's life. Her health care experience helps her add a little medical reality to her stories.

Kat grew up in a large family and feels that family is an important part of her stories. Dynamics between family members can be both a blessing and a curse.

When she is not creating new novel ideas, no pun intended, she can be found baking or enjoying music with a latte. She loves to travel and camp with her husband, Rocky, and dog, Moxie.

Kat can be followed on her Facebook page, *For the Protection of a Woman*, @redkat6350.